"I just hate the way everyone looks at you."

"Do you? Or do you hate the way everyone looks at you when you're with me?"

"Both."

Ryder hadn't expected her to answer so fast. "Chelsea, I'm flattered you've taken the time to do this for me." Ryder didn't want to sound ungrateful, but he didn't want to be her pet project either. "I appreciate everything, but please don't do this again. I'm still trying to figure out why you're risking your reputation. You need to accept me for who I am now. Not who you want me to be tomorrow. Besides, you have a little improvement of your own to do."

"Excuse me? What is that supposed to mean?" Her foot tapped again.

Ryder cursed himself for not keeping that last part to himself. "You told me the other night you don't get out much. You need to make time. Forget the picture-perfect image you seem to compete with, and just be you."

Dear Reader,

Welcome to the last book in my Saddle Ranch, Montana series. Writing this one was bittersweet. While I was delighted to tell Ryder's story, I knew it would be the last time I sat down with the Slade family and the other townsfolk I had grown to love.

Two years ago, I started this journey. Since then I've rescued animals with Harlan and Belle, celebrated Christmas with Dylan and Emma, gone dog sledding with Garrett and Delta, changed lots of diapers with Wes and Jade, and fallen in love with wild horses and donkeys alongside Ryder and Chelsea. I've created many memories living with these characters, and now they'll live on through your time spent with them.

This book is also my last one for what once was Harlequin Western Romance. I found my second home here back in 2012 when it was then known as American Romance. It was here that I discovered my love for writing stories about children...something I never thought I'd enjoy. While this may be the end of Saddle Ridge, I'm not going far. I'll see you soon!

I hope you enjoy *Home on the Ranch: Montana Redemption*. Stop by and visit me at amandarenee.com. I'd love to hear from you.

Happy reading!

Amanda Renee

HOME *on the* RANCH

MONTANA REDEMPTION

⚒

AMANDA RENEE

⟨H⟩ HARLEQUIN® HOME ON THE RANCH

Recycling programs
for this product may
not exist in your area.

ISBN-13: 978-1-335-47490-2

Home on the Ranch: Montana Redemption

Copyright © 2019 by Amanda Renee

Printed in U.S.A.

www.Harlequin.com

Amanda Renee was raised in the northeast and now wriggles her toes in the warm coastal Carolina sands. Her career began when she was discovered through Harlequin's So You Think You Can Write contest. When not creating stories about love and laughter, she enjoys the company of her schnoodle, Duffy, as well as camping, playing guitar and piano, photography and anything involving animals. You can visit her at amandarenee.com.

Books by Amanda Renee

Harlequin Western Romance

Saddle Ridge, Montana

The Lawman's Rebel Bride
A Snowbound Cowboy Christmas
Wrangling Cupid's Cowboy
The Bull Rider's Baby Bombshell

Harlequin American Romance

Welcome to Ramblewood

Betting on Texas
Home to the Cowboy
Blame It on the Rodeo
A Texan for Hire
Back to Texas
Mistletoe Rodeo
The Trouble with Cowgirls
A Bull Rider's Pride
Twins for Christmas

Visit the Author Profile page
at Harlequin.com for more titles.

For Ashley.

May you run wild and free in the heavens above.

Chapter 1

A backbreaking day on the ranch was better than his best day in prison. Ryder Slade welcomed hard work after getting paroled a week earlier. Unfortunately, his body had forgotten the punishing side of ranch life and he'd pay for it later. He wouldn't complain though. It may be in his job description to help rescue and care for animals at the Free Rein Wild Horse and Donkey Sanctuary, but they were rescuing him. So was his ex-wife, Tori James.

Despite their divorce and her subsequent remarriage, Tori had remained his dearest friend. She'd stood by him during his five-and-a-half-year stint behind bars, when most of his family had kept their distance. Not that he blamed them. After all, he'd been sentenced to ten years for killing his father. Confessing to involuntary manslaughter had been the best and worst decision he'd ever made. It had also had more consequences than he'd ever imagined.

"How are you doing out here?" Tori braked beside him and handed him a bottle of water through the window of her seen-better-days pickup.

Ryder used the bottom of his T-shirt to wipe the sweat from his brow, then thirstily twisted off the cap. "Thank you." He took a long swig as he gazed out over the couple hundred acres his ex-wife had purchased after his incarceration. "I'm almost finished replacing this post, then I'll head in. What time did you say the hay delivery was coming?"

Tori checked her watch. "Around four, so you have an hour. I'm on my way to pick up Missy from school, but I should be back by then. And Nate will be home this weekend, so he can help you replace the remaining fence posts."

He still couldn't believe Tori's husband of two years had agreed to allow Ryder to live and work on the ranch while he stayed out on the road as a long-haul truck driver. "There's more than a weekend's worth of fencing to repair. For now, I'm choosing the absolute worst ones to keep the cost down."

Free Rein operated on a bare-bones budget, relying mostly on donations and adoption fees. That lack of funding affected his wallet too, but housing was a condition of his parole for the next three years and that meant more to him than a decent paycheck. Besides, Tori had been the only person in Saddle Ridge willing to hire him. Moving back to his hometown in northwestern Montana gave him a better chance to salvage any relationship he had left with his family…if a chance even existed.

"I'm making tuna-noodle casserole for dinner, so be sure to come up to the house for a plate later."

Ryder's mouth watered at the mere mention of his favorite dish. His mother had given Tori the recipe along with many others on their wedding day with a note reading: *The way to a man's heart is through his stomach.*

"We've already gone over this." Ryder tightened his grip on the water bottle, almost crushing it. "As much as I appreciate the invite, you're not responsible for feeding me."

"It's the least I can do after the sacrifices you've made."

Ryder ground his back teeth. "Let's not go there."

"Fine, I won't force you to discuss it, but I wish you'd acknowledge what you've done." A worn belt screeched under the hood of her truck. "And there's another item on my list of things to do."

"I can replace it for you," Ryder said, grateful for the subject change.

"I just may take you up on that offer if Nate doesn't get to it on Saturday." She reached for her phone and typed in a note before tossing it onto the passenger side of the worn bench seat. "As I was saying, I don't know anyone who would throw away their life for a crime they didn't commit."

A chill ran down his spine at the memory of that fateful night. "Tori, please. You promised to drop it. I can't risk someone else finding out. Not even Nate."

Tori paled at the mention of her husband. "About that."

"You didn't." Ryder gripped the pickup's window-sill. "How could you?"

"Because Nate wouldn't have agreed to you moving into the old bunkhouse unless I told him the truth." Tori's amber eyes blazed, almost matching the fiery color of her hair. "We have a solid marriage and I want it to stay that way. But what man wouldn't question his wife's motivation for wanting to hire her ex-husband, let alone give him a place to stay? You can trust Nate."

Like I trusted you to keep my secret. "Go pick up your daughter."

She didn't attempt to explain any further as the truck rolled forward. "I'll see you later."

"Yep," he mumbled as she drove off. An uneasiness settled in his gut. Ryder grabbed the shovel he'd left leaning against the four-wheeler he'd ridden out on earlier and jammed it into the ground, breaking open a blister on his palm. His newfound freedom threatened to destroy everything he had managed to protect. Now his families' fate rested in Nate's hands. A man he'd only met a few times when Tori visited him in prison. He seemed nice enough on the surface, but could he be trusted?

An hour later, Ryder stood on the back of a flatbed truck, tossing one hay bale after another onto a smaller tractor rack he'd driven into the barn to off-load. At almost seventy pounds apiece, they were more of a work-out than anything he'd done in prison. How had Tori managed to run the ranch while Nate was away with only a handful of volunteers?

A child's laughter echoed in the barn's entrance as a flash of blonde hair tore past him. "You'll never catch me," she sang as she rounded the front of the truck.

"Hey, kid!" Ryder called out as he tossed another bale. He looked around for Tori and Missy. The girl couldn't be over nine or ten years old. "You can't play here. It's too dangerous."

"Who is that?" the feed driver asked from the rack as he straightened the bales Ryder threw down to him.

"Maybe she's one of Tori's daughter's friends." They were close to the same age, although Missy had been deaf since birth and unable to speak that well; this girl sang as clear as the wind. After off-loading the top row, Ryder jumped down and worked on the next. "Where did she go? I don't see her."

"I think she's under the bed." The driver crouched down. "Nope, not there."

Ryder released the last set of straps and continued to off-load when the girl began singing again. He looked at the driver. "I thought you said she wasn't under there." He leaned forward, trying to see over the side without tipping the bales. "Get out before you get hurt."

"She must have been hiding behind the tires." He shrugged and called to the girl as Missy ran past the truck. "Is that the deaf kid?"

Ryder halted midlift and set the bale down. "Her name is Missy, and yes, she's deaf." He was fairly certain the driver hadn't meant anything derogatory by his remark, but Ryder was extremely protective of the girl he'd help raise until his arrest. He'd been there the day Missy was born, much to the dismay of Tori's boyfriend at the time. Good thing Ryder had been because the jerk took off the minute Missy failed the newborn hearing test.

He'd learned sign language alongside Tori and even married her so she wouldn't struggle as a single parent. He loved them both, but he'd never been in love with Tori. When their marriage finally fell apart, Ryder felt he'd let them both down.

Ryder waved his arms to get Missy's attention. When she looked his way, he attempted to sign before realizing he still had on his heavy work gloves. He tugged them off and heard the other girl's laughter again before seeing her head poke out from under the bed between the truck and the rack.

"Kid!" When she didn't flinch at the sound of his voice, Ryder assumed she was deaf, as well. The side of his body hit the bales as he jumped off the flatbed, causing a three-high stack to lean.

"Watch out!" the driver shouted.

Ryder turned to see the blonde girl's back to him, oblivious to the danger inches above her head. He wrapped his hand around her arm and yanked her out of the way a split second before the entire stack crashed to the ground, almost crushing her. She screamed, and Ryder worried he'd inadvertently hurt her. He spun her around to face him and signed, "Are you okay?"

Blue eyes wild, she said, "Yes," without signing in return.

Missy ran between them signing, "We're sorry. Please don't tell my mom."

"I have to," Ryder signed. "I need to tell her parents, too."

"No, my mom will get mad at me," the blonde girl spoke as she signed.

"What's your name?" Ryder asked.

"Peyton." She finger-spelled each letter before demonstrating her name sign.

"My name is Ryder. I'll tell your mom it was an accident, but you have to promise to be more careful." He turned to Missy. "And you know better."

"There they are." Tori saw the fallen bales and rushed to the girls. "Did they do this?"

"No, but Peyton could have been crushed," Ryder said.

Tori signed wildly to her daughter. "How many times have I told you not to play near the outbuildings or the animals if me or Nate aren't around?" She turned to Ryder without waiting for Missy to respond. "What happened?"

The driver groaned as he climbed onto the truck bed and began to off-load the hay alone. Ryder had too much work to do for a lengthy blow-by-blow. "I'll let Missy and Peyton tell you and I'll fill you in on any missing details when I'm done here." He watched them walk away and thought about how lucky Peyton had been as he adjusted his back-support belt and grabbed the first fallen bale, forgetting his hands were bare. The sharpness of the baling wire bit into his blistered palms as he swore under his breath. He yanked his gloves from his back pocket and tugged them on as the truck driver laughed at him. "What's so funny?"

"Are you sure you're cut out for this? Working on a ranch is tough."

"I grew up on one, thank you." Ryder spat, annoyed at the insinuation he was too soft for the job. "I've just been away from it for a while. Give me time." He was a patient man and prison had strengthened his determination. Nothing would stop him from regaining his life and earning his family's forgiveness.

Nothing.

Chelsea Logan enjoyed her evening drives to the horse sanctuary to pick up her daughter, Peyton. Seeing the wild mustangs run across the lush green pastures as she turned onto the ranch road was the stress relief she needed after a drama-filled day in family court. While most of her clients' time spent before a judge set the steadiest of nerves alight, today had been particularly rough. Watching a parent lose custody because they couldn't earn enough to support their child rankled her to the core. Especially when the ex-spouse had erected one roadblock after another. But, those injustices would make her fight twice as hard when she appealed the ruling.

A rescued burro brayed near the adoption center as she parked her Chevy Impala in front of the corral fence. She stepped out of the car and inhaled the scent of fresh-cut hay. It was only the third week of September, but snow already dappled the majestic Swan Range in the distance. She and Peyton had moved to Saddle

Ridge a year ago from the bustling metropolis of Helena and she still hadn't found the time to explore the area.

She reached into her car for her bag when a pair of nice-fitting Wranglers and a Stetson caught her attention through the window. "Oh, that's definitely not Nate," she murmured as she watched the man saunter toward the barn. She stood for a better view and sucked in a breath as he turned toward her. Between his chiseled jawline and broad chest, she didn't know where to look first. Instead, she settled on his belt buckle, which was a mistake when he followed where her eyes landed. The wave of heat warmed her cheeks as a slow, easy smile spread across his face. *Have mercy.*

"Mama!" Peyton ran across the yard and hugged her tight. Instantly, she knew her daughter had done something wrong since her normal greeting consisted of a shrug and sometimes a wave if Chelsea was lucky.

Chelsea tried to set Peyton at arm's length, but her daughter refused to let go. A tactic she had learned after losing her hearing. In her daughter's mind, she couldn't get in trouble if Chelsea was unable to sign to her. Before she could pry Peyton's fingers from her back and find out what had happened, the man had closed the distance between them.

"Good evening." He touched the brim of his hat in greeting. "I'm Ryder. You must be Peyton's mom."

He was even more attractive up close. Blue eyes the color of a glacier pool coupled with a hint of sandy blond hair gave him a James Dean vibe that made her toes curl inside her high-heeled sling-backs.

"It's nice to meet you, Ryder. I'm Chelsea. I'd shake

your hand, but I don't think my daughter will let me."
Thank God for small favors. She shook hands all day
with people, yet she suspected Ryder's touch would
leave her wanting more. Maybe it was time to download
a dating app because drooling over her friend's ranch
hand could only lead to trouble. "Are you new here?"
Peyton lifted her head to look at Chelsea, most likely
sensing the reverberations from her voice. When she
saw Ryder, her eyes widened. Uh-oh. Peyton had definitely done something wrong.

"I started a few days ago, but I've known Tori for a
lifetime and then some. I've mostly been working on the
other side of the ranch. I met your daughter for the first
time this afternoon." He knelt on one knee beside Peyton and signed as he spoke. "I need to explain to your
mother what happened. Don't worry, it will be okay."

Chelsea groaned and freed herself from Peyton's
stronghold, allowing her to use her hands. "What did
she do?"

"Missy and Peyton were playing near the barn while
I was off-loading hay from a flatbed. A stack of bales
fell off the truck and almost hit her. She didn't get hurt,
but it gave her a good scare."

Chelsea forced the fear that grew deep within her to
remain at bay. Ever since Peyton had gone deaf three
years ago because she'd contracted osteomyelitis after
surgery for a broken leg, Chelsea couldn't stress enough
how important it was to always be aware of her sur-
roundings.

"What did I tell you when we first came here?" she
asked Peyton.

"Not to wander around the ranch."

Chelsea blew out a breath in frustration. "You need to sign when you speak. It's the only way you'll improve." The teachers had already cautioned her that Peyton's lazy signing would become a hindrance as she got older.

An eye roll was Peyton's only response.

"Okay, that's not helping the situation. We'll discuss this later." She returned her attention to Ryder and continued to sign. "I appreciate you telling me what happened. I apologize, and I'll pay for any damage."

Ryder rose, standing close enough for her to touch him, but not nearly as close as she would like. *Good Lord, it's been too long since I've been on a date.*

"There wasn't any. And it was an accident. Right, kiddo?" He winked at Peyton. "Tori told me the feed deliveries usually come in the morning, so this was probably the first time your daughter's been here for it. It was an honest mistake."

"I appreciate your understanding." She wrapped an arm around Peyton's shoulder. "Thank you."

"My pleasure. I hope to see you soon." He tipped his hat briefly before walking away.

Chelsea averted her eyes from the magnificent view of him leaving and returned her attention to Peyton. "I'm glad you're all right, but you need to be more careful. I can't watch you twenty-four hours a day."

The corners of Peyton's mouth turned slightly upward. She was doing her best not to smile and Chelsea didn't find humor in the situation. Being a single parent was hard enough—raising a child who was still adjusting to being deaf and learning to communicate all over again was even harder.

"Chelsea." Tori ran down the walkway toward them. "I'm assuming Ryder filled you in on what happened. I'm so sorry. The phone rang and when I went to answer it, they took off. I figured they were in the stables and headed down there when I heard Ryder trying to warn Peyton. I should have told him there was another deaf child around."

"I understand." Chelsea's concern began to subside. "I don't expect you to have eyes on them nonstop. They're kids, and they want to play. They know better though. This was on them." She signed to Peyton, "Let's get your things and head home."

Riding in a car with Peyton always proved challenging. Her daughter could chatter away in the back seat, but Chelsea couldn't respond…at least not fully. Ryder was proficient in signing and she wondered if he had learned for Missy's benefit. She wanted to drill Tori about him, beginning with *is he single* followed by *doesn't your husband mind*?

"Missy said Ryder and her mom used to be married."

That got Chelsea's attention. "Really? Wow." Chelsea signed with her right hand.

"He just got out of jail, so Mrs. James gave him a job."

Chelsea braked hard, twenty feet before the stop sign. She twisted in her seat to face Peyton. "What do you mean he just got out of jail?"

"Missy said he killed his dad and has been away for a long time."

The sound of a car horn behind them startled Chelsea. She had a million more questions she wanted to ask her daughter, but they'd have to wait until they got home.

Forget that! She wasn't about to wait for an explanation. She pulled over, allowing the other car to pass as she pressed the phone button on her steering wheel. "Call Tori."

"Calling Pizza."

Crap! Chelsea disconnected the call. She pushed the button again as Peyton continued to tell her about her day. "Call Tori."

"Calling Mom." *Oh, come on!* She ended the call, waved her hand to get Peyton's attention and brought a finger to her lips, signaling for her to be quiet.

"Third time's the charm." She tried again. "Call Tori."

"Calling Tori."

Chelsea inhaled deep, trying to calm down as she waited for Tori to answer. How could she allow a man like that near Peyton or even her own daughter?

"Hey, Chelsea." Tori's voice boomed through the car speakers.

"Peyton just told me something about Ryder and I need to know if it's true. Was he just released from prison for killing his father?"

"Yes, but—"

"But nothing." How dare she have the nerve to make excuses! "I realize you can hire whoever you want, but you had an obligation to tell me."

Tori paused before responding, leaving Chelsea to wonder if she'd hung up on her. "Hello?"

"I'm here." Tori sighed. "You're right. I should have. But Ryder Slade isn't who everyone makes him out to be."

"Ryder Slade? How do I know that name?" *Slade.* "Is he related to Harlan Slade, one of the deputy sheriffs in town?"

"They're brothers."

In the rearview mirror, Chelsea watched Peyton touch the speaker next to her head and detect the sound vibrations were from a phone conversation and not music. "Who are you talking to?"

Chelsea shook her head and continued her conversation with Tori. "Peyton said Ryder killed their father."

"Accidentally."

"I don't care if it was an accident or not." Tori's casualness began to irk her further. "How long has he been in prison?"

"Five and a half years."

"Oh, good Lord. And let me guess, he's out on parole."

"Yes. He needed a job and a place to live—"

"He's living with you?" How much worse could this get? "Your husband's okay with this?"

"I'm sorry." Tori's tone thickened with sarcasm. "That's none of your business. I apologized for not telling you about Ryder. And I should have informed you before he arrived, but as for my relationship with him or my husband, that's off-limits."

"Fine, but Peyton's not allowed over there again."

Chelsea jabbed the steering wheel's phone button, ending their conversation.

Fifteen minutes later, she pulled into their driveway and parked, almost forgetting to unfasten her seat belt as she got out. How dare Tori allow an ex-convict near her nine-year-old daughter. She shoved her key in the front door so hard, she was surprised when it didn't snap in half. Peyton grabbed the mail from the box before following her into the house. Not bothering to even take off her jacket, Chelsea dropped her briefcase and bag on the floor and beelined for her desk on the other side of their small craftsman-style living room.

Answers. She needed answers.

She flipped open her laptop and fumbled for the power button. Just great. Now she had to tell her daughter she couldn't go to Missy's anymore. She hated to leave her in the after-school program and dreaded the fallout. Peyton was crazy about the sanctuary's rescued horses and donkeys. They fed her dream to become an equine vet one day. She started talking about them at breakfast and didn't stop until her head hit the pillow at night. Hearing loss wouldn't hold her child back from reaching for the stars. Now Chelsea had to be the bad guy and take away the thing her daughter loved most.

They hadn't had these problems when they'd lived in Helena. Her parents had watched Peyton every day after school, and most nights they'd had dinner over there too. It had been the perfect arrangement until the deaf school closed. Without another school nearby, Chelsea had been forced to move. When a law firm in Saddle Ridge near the highest-rated deaf school in the state made her a lucrative offer, she jumped on it. The four-hundred-mile move away from family and the only place they'd ever lived had been tough on Peyton. It took a while for the two of them to adjust, but after renting an apartment for a few months, they'd finally found a home and settled into a solid routine...until today.

"Mama? Are you mad at me?"

She closed her eyes and gripped the edge of the desk. Peyton was too young to understand Chelsea's anger and fear. She turned to her and signed, "No, sweetheart. I'm not mad at you. I love you." Chelsea needed a minute alone to think. "Do you want to help me make dinner tonight?"

"Can we have homemade pizza?" Peyton signed, restoring her faith that her daughter had paid attention to their earlier conversation.

"The dough takes a long time to rise. Do you really want to wait that long?"

"I had a snack at Missy's house. Please, Mama. We haven't made it in months."

"Okay, you're in charge of the menu tonight. Go find the recipe and get all the ingredients ready. I'll be in to help you in a few minutes."

Peyton spun around and skipped out of the room, giving Chelsea a chance to do a little research on Ryder Slade.

Within seconds, the screen filled with hundreds of search results. Numerous articles detailed the events that had occurred the night of his father's death. Ryder and Tori's marriage had just ended, and he had drowned his sorrows at a bar. Tori picked him up and drove him home, where an argument ensued with his father, resulting in Ryder getting behind the wheel of a truck and running him over. Frank Slade had been pronounced dead at the scene. Ryder confessed to involuntary manslaughter and had been sentenced to ten years in prison. He had just become eligible for parole last month.

Chelsea scanned article after article, the most recent from the morning of his release last week. Her hands shook as she logged on to the county website and entered his name. Two pages' worth of charges from his late teens and early twenties filled the screen. Nothing serious. Mostly disorderly conduct, speeding and trespassing. But it was enough to show a pattern of bad behavior.

Regardless, he had killed a man, spent time in prison and there was no way her daughter was going anywhere near Ryder Slade ever again.

Chapter 2

The sun had just begun to climb over the Swan Range when he heard Tori's front door slam shut, shattering Ryder's early morning tranquility. He continued to fill the troughs in the donkey corral as Missy stomped down the porch steps toward her mother's pickup. He waved, but instead of a wave in return, she nailed him with a death glare that wordlessly said he was in trouble with the ten-year-old.

When Tori emerged from the house a minute later, he shut off the water and jumped the fence so they could talk, but the slow shake of her head cautioned Ryder not to cross into enemy territory. With a nod in acknowledgment he headed to the donkey barn to turn them out for the day. Even the most hardheaded mule could figure out he was the source of Missy's anger. He'd squealed on her and her friend yesterday and judging by Missy's attitude, one or both had been punished in some way. Tori handled problems by discussing them—at least she had when they'd been together—but he knew nothing about Peyton's mom.

Chelsea.

The woman he couldn't get off his mind. He wanted to believe his incarceration played a role in her filling his every thought. That made the most sense. But he'd passed some beautiful women in town since his release and he hadn't given them so much as a second glance. Chelsea was different. His fingers itched to touch her. His mouth already craved the taste of her kiss.

Maybe it was because she was still a mystery to him. He hadn't seen a ring or telltale tan line of one, so he assumed she wasn't married. And she definitely hadn't been around before he went away. He would have remembered her. She had to be new to town, or at least relatively so. Her long, wavy golden blonde hair reminded him more of California than Montana, making him wonder if she was a West Coast transplant. Chelsea on the beach wearing nothing but a bikini would make any man drop to their knees in surrender. She wasn't what he would call a skinny woman, but she sure had curves in all the right places. Curves he would never feel. Because no matter how attracted he was to her, he wasn't about to test his relationship with Tori by trying to date her friend.

Besides, judging by Chelsea's tailored black skirt and cream-colored blouse he'd bet a million dollars was made from silk, she was way out of his league. A woman like her would never get involved with a man out on parole.

After releasing the donkeys and horses into their respective pastures, Ryder saddled Tori's horse, Sadie. He ran his hand down the side of the animal's neck, missing his own horse. His mom had sold him, along with the family ranch, shortly after his father's death. At the very least, she could have given Dante to one of his brothers or his uncle after the sacrifice he'd made. He'd like to say guilt had played a role, but he still wasn't sure if his mother remembered that fateful night. He hadn't spoken to or seen her since his sentencing. And even then, she had been mostly despondent.

Ryder led Sadie from the stables just as Tori's truck turned onto the ranch road. His morning ride would have to wait a few more minutes while he found out what was going on with Missy.

"I see I've already made an enemy out of your daughter," Ryder said as he crossed the dusty parking area with Sadie in tow.

"Unfortunately, she isn't your only enemy." Tori hopped from the truck and slammed the door behind her. "Chelsea Logan is furious I let you anywhere near her daughter. She refuses to allow Peyton to come here anymore."

Ryder's stomach tightened. He'd expected some fallout from yesterday, but not this. "What happened? What did she say?" Not that it mattered. He was an ex-con fresh from prison.

"Not much. When they left here Peyton told Chelsea who you were and where you've been. She called me on her way home, asking if it were true. I said yes, and before I had a chance to explain she tore into me and even went as far as questioning how Nate feels about you." Tori's eyes narrowed. "Can you believe her nerve? Let me tell you, I had a few things to say about that and then she said Peyton couldn't come over anymore. And that's fine. You would think a lawyer of all people would take a moment to listen to both sides of the story."

"Chelsea's a lawyer?" Ryder groaned. By now she'd probably read about every last detail of his criminal past. And that bothered him. It shouldn't, but it did. A record like his was impossible to hide. But the police report had clearly stated his father's death had been an accident. "Maybe things will be better today. It's not as if I had maliciously set out to kill my father."

"You didn't kill him, period." Tori stomped her foot, spooking Sadie.

"Easy, girl," Ryder soothed as he rubbed the horse's muzzle. "Leave it alone, Tori."

"It was one thing when you were still in jail. But you're out now and I don't see how you can live a full life here in Saddle Ridge when everyone believes you killed Frank. You should've never covered for—"

Ryder had had enough. He grabbed Sadie's saddle horn and mounted before Tori finished her sentence. "I think it's best if I find someplace else to work and stay. You're too close to this."

Tori reached for Sadie's halter, stopping him from riding off. "You can't leave."

Ryder leaned forward and covered her hand with his.

"Look at the damage I've already caused. Your friend is furious with you. And Missy hates me."

"She could never hate you."

"Missy was four and a half when I went to prison. She's lived longer without me than she has with me. I'm sure she has more memories with Nate and that's the way it should be. He's her father now." Ryder released her hand and sat back in the saddle, studying Tori. When had their relationship gotten so complicated? "You of all people know our divorce damn near destroyed me. We only got married so Missy could have a home. I had one job and I couldn't make us work. How was I supposed to walk away from the little girl I'd helped raise as my own? I didn't want to be a part-time dad. Not in this small town where I'd inevitably run into you and Missy. My heart couldn't have handled that. Prison made it easier."

"How can you say that?"

"Because it gave me a chance to heal." Even though those old wounds were beginning to open again. "It gave you a chance to find someone new and until a few days ago, Missy had a normal life. I came back into the picture and she's lost her best friend. My being here makes things worse. Not better. I'll finish out the rest of the week and then I'm gone."

"And go where? No one else will hire you. If you walk away from here, you'll go directly to jail. Don't make me call your parole officer."

Ryder laughed at the threat. She wouldn't call just like he wouldn't quit without having another job in place. But that had always been their relationship...

a constant game of taunts and empty threats. It had worked in their friendship but had suffocated the marriage. "You can hire someone else."

"They won't work for what I pay you."

"Now I get it. You only like me because I'm cheap."

The corners of Tori's mouth lifted at the remark. "Even if I could afford to pay you more, your salary would still be lower than what I could offer anyone else because you live on the ranch. I don't trust a stranger around my daughter. It's difficult enough communicating with a ten-year-old. You're able to talk to her when none of the other hands and volunteers can, and she loves you despite her attitude this morning."

Tori still knew how to tug at his heartstrings. The headache that had been brewing at the base of his skull had worked its way between his eyes. He pinched the bridge of his nose, willing himself not to cave in to her guilt trip.

"Besides, both Nate and I feel better having you on the ranch when he's on the road. It allows him to take longer hauls without having to rush home every other day. He trusts me with you. And he trusts you with us. If you leave, you'll be hurting my family. I need you to stand by your commitment."

Guilt trip launched and on target. "Okay, I'll stay… for now."

"Good. Then get to work. I'm not paying you to sit and look pretty on a horse all day."

She slapped Sadie's rear, setting her off into a gallop. He tightened the reins and squeezed his thighs to regain control of the horse, bringing her to a canter.

"Nice, Tori. Real nice," he called over his shoulder. Her laughter ricocheted off the stables, mocking him. And he wouldn't have it any other way. They may not be a family anymore, but they were friends. Both she and Nate were the only ones who treated him like a human instead of an inmate.

After he'd decided not to eat dinner with Tori and Missy last night, Ryder had headed into town for a bite. Alone. Those scenes in a movie where someone walks into a room and the whole place falls quiet…they were real. All eyes had been on him when he entered the Iron Horse Bar & Grill. He'd recognized just about everyone there, and except for a few nods and brim touches, they'd ignored him.

It would have been the perfect time to call Harlan, the only one of his four brothers who had visited him in prison. And while those visits had been few and far between, at least Harlan had tried. That was why it surprised him his brother hadn't reached out to him since his release. The parole board had notified his family since they were *victims* of his crime. He'd been shocked when they hadn't shown up for his parole hearing or provided impact statements to block his release. That led him to believe they had possibly forgiven him. But after a week, they still hadn't contacted him, and he wasn't about to force the issue. Tori had done her best to get them together. She told them where he was living, and she'd given him a phone, preprogrammed with his family's numbers. If they were ready to talk to him, they would have contacted him…and vice versa. It wasn't time yet.

He dug his phone out of his shirt pocket, tapped the web browser button and typed… Chelsea Logan Saddle Ridge, Montana. Within seconds, her photo and the law office where she worked appeared on the screen. He saved the photo and added her number to his contacts. His thumb hovered over the call button before clearing the screen and pocketing the phone. What he needed to say had to be said in person. And the thought of seeing Chelsea made his day all that much better. She may hate him now, but he'd find some way to change her mind…for Missy and Tori's sake.

"Swipe right if you're interested in the guy, swipe left to pass," Jocelyn explained to Chelsea during lunch downtown. They had just finished setting up Chelsea's profile on the dating app Jocelyn had talked her into downloading. "Eventually if you swipe right on enough people, you'll get a match. Then you can send him a message and start a private chat. If you hit it off, you can make plans to meet…someplace public."

Chelsea looked up from her phone. "I don't know about this. I'm not ready to start seeing anyone yet."

"No one says you have to. If the person is from Saddle Ridge, you may already know him."

"Or represent him." Chelsea swiped left on a newly divorced client of hers. Asking her friend about a dating app had gone way beyond answering a few questions. Now her face and dating must-haves were out there for the world to see. Another man appeared on the screen. Attractive. Professional. No kids. Never married. Similar interests. And the total opposite of Ryder

Slade. She swiped left. Photo after photo of eligible men and none did *it* for her. If she could only define *it*, she'd be set. The perfect man didn't exist. The wrong man did. She'd experienced the wrong one many times over. The bad boys with records. The ones she thought she could reform and turn into Mr. Perfect. Just as a leopard couldn't change his spots, a bad boy couldn't turn good. Instead of a *rebel without a cause*, she needed a Sheriff Andy Taylor. She swiped left again.

"Just choose one already." Jocelyn nudged her arm. "This is why you're still single. You're too picky."

"You're single, too." Chelsea set down her phone. "Between my schedule and Peyton, I don't have time to go out."

"I may be single, but I have a date tomorrow night." She grabbed Chelsea's phone. "I'll find you someone and we'll make it a double. It'll take the pressure off."

"Give me that!" Chelsea reached across the table, almost spilling her glass of water. "Even if I wanted to, I don't have a babysitter anymore."

"What happened to Tori?" Jocelyn handed her the phone. "I thought she loved watching Peyton."

"Yesterday I found out she has a freshly released ex-con working and living on her ranch."

Jocelyn grinned. "Ah, Ryder." She clucked her tongue. "What I wouldn't give to swipe right on him."

"Are you serious?" Jocelyn's obvious attraction to the cowboy made her pulse accelerate…but only out of concern for her friend. Because what other reason could there be? "Have you seen his rap sheet?"

"I've heard about it. That whole thing with him had

happened before I moved here, but my sister is close with his family and I've represented them before."

"You're a public defender. The only way you could have represented them was if one or more of them had been arrested." Chelsea shook her head and sighed. "Is breaking the law a family trait?"

"It's not like that. The Slades are good people with big hearts. If there is anything this job has taught us, it's to always look beneath the surface." Jocelyn reached for her bag and tossed a twenty on the table before rising. "I have fifteen minutes to get to court. And don't worry. I won't date your cowboy. I'll leave him intact for you."

"Oh, very funny." Chelsea tugged a few bills from her wallet. "Thanks for meeting me for lunch."

"Swipe right a few times and maybe we can do it again with dates."

Chelsea threw her napkin across the table. "Get out of here before Judge Sanders holds you in contempt."

"You know he's related to the Slades, don't you?"

"No, I didn't."

"Deputy Sheriff Harlan Slade is his son-in-law." Jocelyn slung her bag over her shoulder. "Okay, I have to fly. Ciao."

A judge, a sheriff, a jailbird and apparently someone else who'd been arrested. Definitely not a family she wanted to get involved with. Too much drama. She paid the bill and checked her watch. She had another hour before she met with her next client. A simple adoption case. The rest of her afternoon should be fairly low-key and that was just the way she liked it. Simple. Quiet.

Boring.

Okay, maybe Jocelyn was right. The most excitement she'd had lately had been buying the shoes she wore today. There was no harm in chatting with a guy or two. Chelsea reopened the dating app once she got outside the restaurant. After swiping left on the first four men, she hesitated on the fifth. "He looks nice."

"Nah, too high maintenance. I'd swipe left," a male said over her shoulder, his breath close enough to graze her cheek.

"What the—" Chelsea spun to face the man, almost twisting her ankle in the process. "Oh, ouch."

His hands wrapped around her upper arms to steady her. Strong muscular hands that had no business being anywhere on her body. "Are you all right? I didn't mean to startle you."

"I'm fine." She pushed away from him. "What do you want?" And damn, did he look fine.

"I was on my way to your office when I saw you." His eyes traveled the length of her, stopping on her new pair of scarlet pumps. "Are you sure you're okay?"

Chelsea had never felt more naked while fully dressed. Her legs, though covered almost to the knee, felt exceptionally bare. Her skin burned under his gaze as his eyes rose to meet hers.

"Yes, thank you." She squared her shoulders. "What can I do for you, Mr. Slade?"

"For starters, please call me Ryder. Mr. Slade was my dad."

"The man you killed." For a woman who prided herself on remaining civilized no matter how audacious opposing counsel could sometimes be, she cringed at her own words. "I'm sorry. That was rude of me."

"Yeah, it sure was." Ryder took a step back. "Regardless, I'm not here for my benefit. I'm here for Tori and Missy. Missy especially. And no, they did not ask me to come see you."

A smart retort threatened to break free, but she gnawed on the side of her cheek instead. What was it about Ryder that unsettled her so easily? "Go on."

"Tori did me a huge favor by giving me a job and a place to stay. Especially after she informed me no one else around was willing to hire me." Ryder tilted his hat, exposing more of his face. A hint of pain and regret reflected in his eyes. "I'm grateful for their help but it's far from ideal. You have every right not to want your daughter around someone like me. I don't want my presence to come between you and Tori or Missy and Peyton."

"I'm sure you didn't, but—"

"Please allow me to finish. I offered to leave the ranch after I found out about the argument you two had."

"Leave as in quit and move out?" A change like that would surely affect his parole. As an attorney, she couldn't allow him to jeopardize his freedom that way. "Wasn't that job a condition of your release?"

"Yes, and Tori's already threatened to turn me in to my parole officer if I do, so please don't join that club."

"I would never tell you to do that. I mean, yes, I said some things to Tori last night that I probably shouldn't have said. And I won't pretend that I haven't read your police record or researched your plea deal." She lifted her eyes to his, almost afraid to see him for who he was today, not the impersonal man she'd read about. He may have been guilty as sin, but a lot could be said about someone who faced their crimes head-on. "I respect the decisions you've made regarding your case and I wouldn't want you to return to prison. But that doesn't mean I'm comfortable with you being around my daughter. I'll talk to Tori. If she'll forgive me for the way I treated her, maybe the girls can see each other outside the ranch."

"I appreciate that, but I had something else in mind. Until I find another job, and someone more suited to take my place at Free Rein, I thought you and I could come to a compromise. I'll make myself scarce whenever Peyton's around. You won't have to worry about me anymore."

Ryder's willingness to bend for her benefit was slightly annoying...and sweet. "Why does it matter to you?"

"I'm not sure how much Tori told you about our marriage, but I raised Missy as my own until the divorce. Yes, I've made more than my share of mistakes, but I've also worked hard to change. My life wasn't always a mess. I had a successful business training horses until the night...the night my dad...died." The last word was barely a whisper as his eyes shimmered with wetness. "It was an accident. My dad fell behind the truck. There was no way to see him from the driver's seat. An—and then it was too late."

His admission, given so openly, settled over her, and compassion for him bloomed. "Ryder, I'm so sorry."

Chelsea reached for him, wanting to comfort him. Her hand rested against his chest and he covered it with his own. His heart pounded beneath her fingertips and she pressed her palm harder against him to feel its power. She cleared her throat and slid from his grasp, determined to maintain control. "Your confession hadn't conveyed your anguish, and I hadn't even thought to take it into consideration until now. That must have been the worst night of your life."

"That night not only destroyed my family, it turned Missy's world upside down." Ryder exhaled slowly and rubbed the back of his neck as if trying to regain his own control. "The divorce was bad enough, but no four-year-old should ever have to visit the only father she's ever known behind bars. I told Tori to keep her away. She deserved better. I love that kid with all I am. It kills me to know she's hurting because of something I've done. She's had to make too many adjustments in her life, she doesn't need to make one more where Peyton is concerned."

Okay, he made a compelling argument. His priors had only been misdemeanors from his late teens and early twenties, and she found his love for Missy endearing. Tori hadn't gone into detail about Missy's biological father, except he'd left right after the baby had been born. That was more than she could say for Peyton's father. He left the day after she told him she was pregnant. It took a big man to step into the role of baby daddy.

"I'll take everything you've said into consideration and I'll give Tori a call, too. Maybe we can work something out." Deep down, though, she knew she'd need time to think all this over. She wasn't completely un-sympathetic toward his situation, but at the end of the day she was a mom, and her daughter's well-being would always come first.

"That's all I ask." Ryder tugged his hat down low. "Enjoy the rest of your day and stay off those dating sites. I did time with some bad people who found their victims on those places. I'm not saying there aren't good guys out there, it's just safer dating a friend of a friend instead."

Chelsea swallowed hard. A friend of a friend? No, he couldn't possibly mean... "I'll keep that in mind."

"I hope you do." He winked and turned to walk away, once again giving her a view she didn't need. Or want. She equated Ryder Slade to a campfire. They were both fun to look at and could even keep her warm for an hour or two. But she wouldn't want to touch one. Nope. The sooner she extinguished Ryder the less likely she was to get burned.

Chapter 3

It hadn't even been twenty-four hours since he'd seen Chelsea and he was already trying to come up with a casual way to run into her. If only to make sure she hadn't swiped right on any strange men. Not that he should care. Well, that wasn't entirely true. He cared from a protective standpoint. No one should endure the horrible treatment some of his former fellow inmates had inflicted on women. Other than that, her personal life was her business. He was only watching out for her considering she was Tori's friend…again.

Yesterday, Tori had briefly mentioned Chelsea had called, but she hadn't elaborated further. She'd been in a dark mood ever since Nate hadn't made it home last night. As of this morning, she still hadn't heard from him. Now almost lunchtime, she hadn't returned to the ranch after she'd dropped Missy off at school. It wasn't like her to blow off her morning routine. He hoped nothing had happened, although he assumed she'd call him if it had. At least it was Friday, and he had help from the sanctuary volunteers that came in and worked every weekend.

The rumble of a big rig on the main road jarred Ryder from Free Rein's usual serenity. Nate's sleeper-cab semi pulled into the ranch followed by a dually pickup towing what he figured had to be a forty-foot-long livestock trailer. Nate parked in front of the house and hopped out the driver's side, the diesel idling behind him as he motioned for the dually to continue along the fence line to the next pasture.

Nate waved Ryder over. Judging by the dark shadows under his eyes, he needed some serious sleep. "We have eighty-two mustangs coming in from a Nevada wild horse roundup. I got them before they were sold for slaughter." Nate glanced around at the empty stalls. "Bring in Chief and Sadie. We need to clear out the south pasture so we can quarantine the incoming horses. There are three more trailers on the way."

"You got it." Ryder snatched a bag of horse treats from the feed room and sprinted toward the main corral. He stopped long enough at the gate to grab a couple lead ropes and then climbed onto the fence rails. Jamming two fingers in his mouth, he whistled loudly. Sadie and Chief lifted their heads from the hay feeder and continued munching, unaware of the job they were about to do. As cutting horses, they'd round up and move the herds out into the north pasture, giving the rescues their freedom. At least as much freedom as they could have on an enclosed sanctuary. He shook the bag and yelled, "cookie, cookie, cookie" just as Tori had shown him to do when it was time for them to come in for dinner. Only they didn't respond to him with the same eagerness. Where was Tori, anyway?

Behind him, another trailer pulled onto the ranch, while Sadie and Chief sauntered toward him. Nothing like a snail's pace when you're in a hurry. Ryder mentally totaled the added feed and hay they would need for the rescues on top of any emergency vet fees. He couldn't even begin to calculate the transportation costs. If the horses had come from the northern Nevada roundups, they'd traveled at least twelve hours to get here.

Ryder whistled again and this time the horses increased their pace. "That's it. Get your cookies." He jumped into the corral and held out the treats. They greedily ate them, allowing him to attach lead ropes to their halters. Nate met him at the fence where they tacked up both horses. "Where's your wife?"

"At the bank trying to get an emergency line of credit," Nate said as he swung into the saddle. "I had to put up my trailer for collateral to get these horses here. If she can't get that loan, I can't get my trailer back. This is the make-or-break point, my friend."

The men rode into the south pasture, quickly moving the existing mustang herds. Normally a herd is comprised of one stallion and eight or so females and their young, but when they sense danger, they form one larger herd for safety. Once Nate and Ryder were confident the pasture was clear, they made a quick perimeter check to ensure there weren't any gaps in the fencing given that a wild horse in a strange environment would look for an escape.

By the time they returned to the horse trailers, volunteers had erected a temporary chute and holding pen. Ryder recognized some people, including Belle Barnes. Or rather Belle Barnes-Slade since she had married his brother Harlan last summer. She waved and smiled—a genuine smile—in his direction as she continued talking to Dr. Lydia Presley, Saddle Ridge's resident large animal veterinarian.

"This will give us a chance to assess each horse without traumatizing them further than they've already been," Nate explained. "You should have seen the pens they were in. They could barely move. They had trampled fallen weaker horses and babies to death."

The sound of horse whinnies and loud thumps filled the air as the horses moved around in the trailers.

"We're ready!" Lydia's husband, Calvin, shouted to Nate above the noise.

"Let's do this." Nate waved his hat, signaling for them to open the first trailer's door. Huddled together, the horses hesitated to break from the herd. Everyone fell silent and remained still as a bay-colored stallion gingerly stepped onto the ramp. His eyes blazed wild with fear as he snorted and stomped his hoof. "You can do it," Nate whispered. "Show them how it's done."

The mustang took another cautious step, giving Lydia a chance to look him over from her side while Calvin did the same from the other. After an approving nod from both, Belle reached through the tubular rails and lightly tapped the horse's rump, causing him to move forward.

Silently, they quickly checked each horse from the first trailer and then moved on to the next. By the time the sun dipped beneath the horizon, they'd off-loaded and freed the final mustang in the south pasture. The rumble of hooves against the ground sounded better than any song Ryder had ever heard on the radio. He'd been a part of something big. Larger than he'd experienced before. Even though he only had a couple dollars to his name and Tori probably wouldn't be able to pay him much of anything after today, it didn't matter. They had saved eighty-two lives. And he'd continue to be a part of their progress as he gained their trust.

The sanctuary strived to train, rehabilitate and adopt out as many wild horses as possible so they could live a full and happy life. Tori and Nate had both warned Ryder his job wouldn't be easy, and he had to admit, the prospect almost seemed daunting. The only experience these horses had had with humans to date had been cruel and inhumane. He'd trained a handful of mustangs before with some success, but this time his life depended on it. They needed one another.

"It's good to see you again."

Ryder jumped at the sound of Belle's voice behind him. He turned to face her, glad that at least one member of his family was talking to him. "You too, Belle."

She reached up and gave him a hug, holding him tight to her. "Welcome home."

Ryder squeezed his eyes shut. Outside of a single hug from Tori the day of his release from jail, a handshake from Nate and Chelsea's sympathetic gesture yesterday, he hadn't felt a genuine human touch since his arrest. "Thank you."

She released him and patted the side of his cheek. "You look good. I know it's Friday night and all, but if you don't already have other plans, I'd like you to swing by the house for dinner and see your niece and nephew. Ivy's eight now and Travis is five-and-a-half months old."

He gave her a small smile, touched at the invite. "I don't think Harlan would approve. I haven't seen or heard from him."

Belle furrowed her brows. "Harlan's been away for over a week at a police training seminar. It came up last minute. He wasn't supposed to go until next month, but someone got sick and he went in their place. I guess he had no way of reaching you before your...your release. He doesn't get home until later tonight. It would be such a great surprise for him when he walks through the door."

Good grief, does she ever come up for air? Ryder tried not to laugh, but he couldn't. "Oh, Belle, it's nice to see some things haven't changed. You're still the chatterbox I remember."

"Ryder Slade, that's the nicest thing you've ever said to me considering you tried to drown me in Flathead Lake when we were kids."

Ryder laughed so hard he snorted. "I did, didn't I. Sorry, kiddo. And yes, I'd love to come to dinner. Are you still a vegan?"

"You know that will never change."

Ryder walked Belle to her truck. "Let me take a

quick shower and then I'll be there. I'm assuming the address hasn't changed."

"No, it hasn't." Belle reached out and gave his hand a sympathetic squeeze. "If there's a special someone you'd like to invite, you're more than welcome to."

"What?" Chelsea's angelic face immediately came to mind after pushing her from his thoughts all afternoon. "I got out of prison a week and a half ago. I assure you there is no one in my life."

"Hmm. Lydia said someone told her you and Chelsea Logan were all cuddly in town yesterday."

"Wow. Rumors spread faster here than they do in the state pen. Chelsea's and Tori's daughters are friends. I've only seen her twice. Once here and once in town. We've had a couple brief conversations, and that's it." Then why did the memory of her warm, soft skin beneath his make the hair on the back of his neck stand at attention? "She's way out of my league."

"From what I hear, Chelsea's extremely down to earth. I don't know her personally, but she has a stellar reputation. She does a lot of pro bono work for single parents and families who can't afford representation."

"Thank you for the info." Ryder cleared his throat. "But I'll pass. I have too much baggage to empty first."

"I'm assuming some of that baggage is your family." Belle slid behind the wheel of her truck. "I can't speak for Dylan, Garrett or Wes but you don't have to worry about your relationship with Harlan. He knows it was an accident."

And Harlan had also questioned if Ryder was hiding the whole truth. "Do me a favor…please tell my brother any discussion about my father's death is off limits. I've answered all the questions and done the time. I can't change that night and as much as I'd love to see my family back together, I've made peace with the fact it may never happen."

His family could disown him a hundred times over and he'd never admit who really drove the truck that killed their father. He'd take that secret to the grave.

A few hours later, Ryder sat idling at the entrance to Harlan's ranch. He'd borrowed Nate's Jeep and picked up a bottle of wine on the way over, but he still hadn't willed the nerve to make it to the front door. The chirp of a siren and the flashing lights in his rearview mirror just about gave him a heart attack until he saw his brother step out the driver's side of the police SUV.

"I'm sorry." Harlan laughed as Ryder jumped off the Jeep's running board. "I wasn't thinking when I did that. I bet sirens and lights are the last thing you need." His brother pulled him into a hug. "It's good to see you, man."

"You have no idea." Ryder clapped him on the back, relieved to finally see one of his brothers. "Thanks for visiting me when I was inside."

Harlan nodded and held him at arm's length, as if taking inventory of him. "I should have visited more often than I did."

"Nah, you didn't owe me anything." Ryder jammed his hands in his pockets. The jeans still stiff from newness, he wondered what had happened to all his clothes and belongings that had been at his parents' house. "How'd you know it was me, anyway?"

"Nate's FRWILD2 plate. Tori has FRWILD1. I couldn't imagine either of them sitting out here too chicken to drive up to the house."

Ryder checked the back of the Jeep. "I hadn't noticed that before. Clever abbreviation for the sanctuary. And for the record, I'm not chicken. Seeing you and Belle is one thing but facing your kid—my niece—after everything that's happened… I just didn't know how to do it."

"Fair enough. Let's go do it together." Harlan gave his brother another hug. "It sure is good to have you home."

"It's good to be here." Ryder held on tight, fighting to forget the loneliness and despair that had been his constant companion for the last five and a half years. "I'm so sorry."

He was sorry for lying to his brother when he had asked him if he'd really been the driver responsible for killing their father. He was sorry for not being able to stop the nightmare that had unfolded that night. And he was sorry his family went through such hell, publicly and privately as they'd had to clean up the mess while he'd been incarcerated.

"Hey," Ryder soothed. "What's going on? You doing okay?" His brother reached in the Jeep and shut it off. "Talk to me."

Ryder struggled to tamp down the overwhelming fear that lived inside him. "I'm good. I'm… Wow. This is harder than I thought it would be."

"What's harder? Talking to me or being out?"

"Being out." Ryder attempted a smile. "How crazy is that? There's no one telling me when to get up or go to bed. I don't have to watch my back constantly, yet I still catch myself doing it. A private shower and bathroom feel like a luxury, even in that old bunkhouse of Tori's. Inside I didn't have to deal with anything except survival. Now that I'm out, I'm seeing people in town I haven't seen in years and I want to say, 'hey let's grab a beer and catch up,' but they want nothing to do with me. Or I'm meeting new people that don't know about my past, but I know they'll find out about it soon enough." An image of Chelsea the first day they'd met drifted into his thoughts. The warmth in her eyes, followed by the anger and disappointment he'd seen the next day when she'd learned the truth…or at least his version. "I didn't have to deal with any of this when I was inside. I hate to say it, but in many ways, it was easier in there."

"I can only imagine. It's not uncommon though. I've arrested people with long histories who want to go back because they feel safer inside. I'm not saying you're one of them, but I do understand. Anytime you want to talk, or not talk and just hang out, call me. It doesn't matter what time. I'm here for you."

"I may take you up on that." His anxiety over tonight had begun to fade some and he felt ready to face whatever came next. "Now how about that dinner your beautiful bride promised me?"

"Knowing my wife, it's quite a spread." Harlan walked back to his SUV. "You'll never know it's vegan. And if she's made her chocolate cake, man oh man, you'll think you've died and gone to heaven."

Ryder never thought he'd see the day Mr. Steak and Potatoes would salivate over vegan chocolate cake... or vegan anything. It proved how the love of a good woman could make anything possible. Again Chelsea came to mind. If only he had a chance of winning her heart the way Harlan had won Belle's.

Chelsea and Peyton climbed the steps of Tori's front porch shortly after eight on Friday night. Normally they'd be home and Peyton would be getting ready for bed, but a few of the partners in Chelsea's law firm had made a sizable donation to the sanctuary after hearing about the mustang rescue this afternoon. Since Tori and Chelsea were friends, they'd asked her to deliver it personally. On any other day, she wouldn't have minded. Today she did.

She hadn't been in the office for five minutes this morning when a senior partner confronted her about Ryder. He had spotted the two of them together on his way to the courthouse and spent a good half hour warning her to stay away from him. By the end of the conversation, she couldn't figure out if he was cautioning her out of the goodness of his heart or if her job would be in jeopardy if she continued her relationship with Ryder. They didn't have a relationship, of course, but Chelsea didn't appreciate her employer interfering in her personal life.

Tori rang the bell and was relieved when Nate answered the door. She figured the chances of Ryder being at the house were slim, but Nate's presence erased those fears.

"Hi, Chelsea. I didn't know you were stopping over." Nate signed as he spoke. Stepping aside, he motioned for them to come in. "What brings you by?"

A man's voice followed by Tori's laughter in the other room stopped Chelsea mid step. Maybe Ryder was there. "I hope I'm not interrupting anything."

"You're not. We just returned from checking on the wild horses we brought in today. Tori's in the kitchen with her brother. Would you like a cup of coffee?"

The tension eased from her body as she followed Nate through the house. "I'd love that."

Nate turned and faced Peyton, walking backward as he signed. "How about a chocolate cupcake and some milk?"

Peyton's face lit brighter than fireworks on the Fourth of July. "Yes, please."

"You said the magic word. Chocolate. She'll be your best friend for life."

Tori rose from the table when they entered the kitchen. "Chelsea, this is a surprise. Is everything okay?"

"Everything's fine. I'm here to drop off a check from my firm. They heard about today and they wanted to make a donation." She removed the envelope from her bag and handed it to Tori. "And there's one from me in there, too. Mine's not much, but I wanted to help in whatever way I could."

Tori tore it open and covered her mouth. "Oh my God." Nate and her brother peered over her shoulder to read the amounts.

"Chelsea, this is extremely generous." Nate wrapped

an arm around his wife's shoulders. "You have no idea how much this means to us."

"I tried getting an emergency credit line increase this afternoon and the bank only gave me a fraction of what we needed. Nate had to put his trailer up for collateral just to cover the transportation costs. This more than makes up the difference." Tori enveloped her in a hug. "Thank you. Thank you so much."

"I'll be sure to tell everyone. I wish I could do more."

"You could always volunteer on the weekends," Tori's brother said.

"Where are my manners?" Tori stuffed the checks back in the envelope and pocketed it. "Chelsea, this is my brother Judd. Judd, this is Chelsea and her daughter, Peyton."

"It's nice to meet you both." He shook their hands. "I didn't mean to put you on the spot like that."

"No, you're right. I should volunteer on the weekends. I'm ashamed I haven't offered before. I don't have a lot of experience with horses, but if you need any clerical assistance in the adoption center or if there is anything both Peyton and I could do together, I'd be willing to help for a few hours a week."

Just as long as it wasn't in Ryder's vicinity. She'd been on an emotional roller coaster ever since she saw him yesterday. Correction…ever since she made the mistake of touching him. The man had gone through hell and her only instinct had been to comfort him. She may be a compassionate woman—she had to be as a family law attorney—but she didn't make a habit out of getting touchy-feely with people.

Nate sat a mug of coffee on the table for Chelsea along with a plate of cupcakes and two glasses of milk. "Missy is in her room. Would you run and get her?" he asked Peyton. She debated for a few seconds as if she wasn't sure her friend was worth waiting an extra few minutes for her cupcake. Choosing friendship over chocolate, she disappeared down the hallway.

"Would you really be willing to volunteer?" Tori asked. "Even after the other day?"

"I'm still not a hundred percent convinced Ryder should be around my daughter." Chelsea pulled out a chair and sat down. "But I appreciated him reaching out to me yesterday and explaining his situation. He doesn't want to come between Peyton and Missy's friendship or ours."

"No, he doesn't. I think once you get to know him, you'll realize he's not the man you think he is."

Chelsea's jaw tightened. That was part of the problem. She didn't want to get to know Ryder. She didn't want to repeat the same mistakes she'd made in the past. As much as she hated to say she had a type, she did. She'd always been drawn to her polar opposite. And Ryder came pretty damn close.

"How about we take the whole Ryder thing one day at a time?"

"I think I can handle that." Tori pushed the plate of cupcakes toward her. "Now eat before the girls get in here and there's nothing left."

For the next few hours, the six of them sat around the kitchen table playing board games and polishing off whatever snacks Tori and Nate had in the house. It wasn't exactly a wild night out on the town, but it felt good spending time with adults outside work. And Judd was a nice enough man. He was single, lived an hour away, had a decent job, and she was completely unattracted to him. The sentiment appeared to be mutual, allowing her to relax and enjoy the company of the opposite sex with zero pressure for it to be something more.

No one had mentioned Ryder's name for the rest of the evening and a part of her couldn't help wondering if he was sitting alone in the bunkhouse. She'd even considered asking Tori if she wanted to invite him, figuring she hadn't included him because she and Peyton were there. But she hadn't and by the time they left, guilt had bored a hole in her stomach. That was until she saw Ryder drive up to the stables in Nate's Jeep. Here she'd felt guilty for hours and he'd had plans.

He waved but made no attempt to come to her. Instead, he stood by the door to the bunkhouse and watched.

Chelsea opened the rear passenger door for Peyton. "Wait here for Mommy. I'll be right back," she quickly signed before closing the door.

The walk across the dirt-covered parking area seemed like miles instead of the hundred yards it was. With each step…each breath…she regretted not getting in the car and driving away. There was no reason for him to be waiting for her and they had nothing left to discuss, yet there they were, face-to-face. So close she could reach out and feel his heart thump against her palm again.

But she didn't.

She couldn't.

Oh, Lord, she wanted to.

"I hope this is a sign you've allowed Peyton and Missy to play together again."

"Tori and I haven't even discussed after school, yet. I had to drop off a donation check from my firm this evening and we ended up staying for a few hours."

Ryder slid his hands in his pockets and leaned against the bunkhouse doorjamb, his hat shielding half of his face from the outdoor wall lantern. "I meant what I said yesterday. I can stay away from any areas Peyton might be when she's here after school."

"I don't doubt that, considering you were working here for a few days before I even saw you. I'm afraid I may have overreacted and for that I apologize. That doesn't mean I still don't have concerns—you can never be too careful when it comes to your kid. But I don't think you want to harm my daughter."

"I would have reacted the same way if the situation had been reversed and we were talking about Missy, not that she's my daughter anymore." Ryder looked past her toward the house. "Tori should have given you a heads-up. That's on her."

She appreciated his honesty and her heart broke for him. In her career, she'd seen many non-biological parents struggle to maintain a relationship with their children when their marriage ended, or their ex moved on with someone else. "Missy is still a part of you, and Tori still wants you involved in her life or else you wouldn't be here."

"On some level she does. I had never adopted Missy.

I'd been there ever since she was born, but she always had Tori's last name, even after we'd married."

"Oh, I didn't realize that. I assumed you had."

"There never seemed to be a reason to make it official. Everyone had accepted I was her father. And then I wasn't. Nate hasn't adopted her either and maybe that's something Tori doesn't want. This way Missy is only ever her daughter." Ryder laughed. "I don't even know why I'm telling you all of this."

She couldn't help but be touched that he was opening up to her. Again, Chelsea wanted to comfort him and take away the pain. "It's all right. We all need someone to talk to. I can't fathom how difficult it must be for you to watch another man parent the daughter you raised for the first four years of her life." For the first time, she saw Ryder for who he was. An outsider—an employee—working for the family that once belonged to him. A lesser man wouldn't have been able to handle it.

Unbiddenly, she found herself even more attracted to him.

"It sure as hell hasn't been easy," he said. "I try not to infringe on their time together even though Tori asks me to join them for dinner almost every night. I don't want to confuse Missy or upset Nate. My sister-in-law invited me to dinner tonight, so I at least got to see part of my family."

"That's wonderful!" Chelsea couldn't help the tiny squeal of delight that escaped her lips. He hadn't been on a date? *Not that it's any of your business.* "How did it go?" She imagined sitting around the table with the people whose father he'd accidentally killed had to have been somewhat strained.

"It was good. I hadn't seen my brother's wife in over ten years. They had dated back in high school and had gone their separate ways until last year. It was nice catching up with Belle and my niece, who wasn't even five the last I saw her. I met my new nephew, who I couldn't get enough of. The little bugger just sucks you in with those big baby blues." Ryder pushed back his hat, giving her full view of his sexy I-can-melt-ice-cream-by-just-looking-at-it smile that flashed across his face. "We're planning to get together again soon."

Chelsea checked over her shoulder to make sure Peyton was all right. She wanted to ask him about his other brothers and his mother, but it was way past her daughter's bedtime. "It sounds like you had a good night. And speaking of good-night, I need to head out."

Ryder uncrossed his feet and pushed off the doorjamb. "Thanks for stopping by and saying hi." He removed his hat and ran his fingers through his thick sandy blond hair, which was a little longer on top than she expected. Now he really looked like James Dean. "Maybe we can grab a drink or a bite to eat sometime."

Did he just ask her out? *I think he did.* Chelsea opened her mouth to say yes and then the earlier conversation with her boss shoved its way to the forefront of her brain. "I don't think that's a good idea. You're Tori's ex-husband and I'm not sure how she would feel about that, especially since she's the only person I have to watch Peyton. I just think it would be awkward asking her to babysit my kid while I'm out with her ex. Besides, I don't really have any free time."

Ryder shrugged. "No, hey, I get it." He tugged his keys from his pocket and slid one into the lock of his door. "Be careful driving home. Good night."

"Thanks." Before she could say *good-night* in return, he shut the door. She ran her fingers lightly over the worn wood, once again remembering the rhythmic drumming of his beating heart. She closed her eyes, willing herself to walk away. But she couldn't. She made a fist and knocked on the door.

Ryder opened it, his shirt unbuttoned and hanging loosely from his jeans. Her eyes immediately fell to the bare skin where her hand had rested yesterday before rising to meet his gaze.

"Yes?" A more arrogant man would have grinned at her obvious stupefaction. Instead, his eyes bore into hers, making her wonder if he could see inside her soul.

"I can't make any promises, but I will talk to Tori and see what she says about…" About what? Her dating Ryder? One drink is not a date. "If she doesn't have a problem with us hanging out, then we'll take it from there." Ugh! Could she have been any vaguer?

His slow, easy smile exposed dimples she hadn't noticed before. "Sounds good."

"Okay then, um, well, good night." *Oh, come on, Chelsea.* She spoke in front of people for a living, yet here she was stumbling over her words like a lovesick teenager.

"Good night, Chelsea."

Guh! The sound of her name on his lips caused every inch of her body to tingle. Before she made more of a fool out of herself, she turned away and walked to her car. When she didn't hear the door close behind her, she knew he was watching. Why couldn't she have worn something a little sexier than a pair of jeans and a sweatshirt? Peyton looked up at her from the car. Because she was the mother of a nine-year-old and she didn't need to wear sexy outfits in front of the ranch hand.

She gave Ryder a quick wave before ducking inside the safety of her car. It, along with her house and job needed to remain Ryder-free zones. She flipped on the interior light and twisted in the seat to face her daughter. "I'm sorry I took so long," she signed.

Peyton smiled. "That's okay, Mommy," she said as she signed.

Chelsea gave her daughter's knee a quick squeeze before turning off the light and starting the engine. Peyton hummed softly. Something she'd done since she'd been a year old. She may not hear her own voice, but she could still feel the vibrations in her mouth and the back of her throat. The tune sounded familiar, but she couldn't place it until her daughter began singing the words.

"Mommy and Ryder, sitting in a tree. K-I-S-S-I-N-G."

Chelsea met her daughter's eyes in the rearview mirror.

"First comes love, then comes marriage, then comes baby in a baby carriage." Peyton giggled before singing the song again.

Chelsea groaned as she pulled onto the main road. So much for her car being a Ryder-free zone.

Chapter 4

Nate reined alongside Ryder, interrupting his memories of last night with Chelsea. Even though he'd only spoken with her for a few minutes, it had felt more intimate than a casual conversation.

"How are they looking?" Nate asked as they watched their new arrivals drink from the creek cutting through the south pasture.

"They're keeping their distance, which is understandable after what they've been through." Ryder despised how the Bureau of Land Management cruelly handled their wild horse roundups. "One of those tourism helicopters flew overhead earlier and spooked them. They probably thought they were being herded again. You might want to contact the helicopter company and see if they'll consider changing their flight pattern or at least fly at a higher elevation. They were way too low for my taste."

"I'll let Tori know."

Ryder nodded as a silence fell between them. He'd never minded company before his incarceration. But after not having a single minute alone for five and a half years, he craved the solitude.

"Are you settling in all right?"

Ryder hesitated before answering, uncertain if Nate asked because he genuinely cared or if he resented him for living and working there. "It's an adjustment. I can never thank you enough for allowing me to stay here. I promise it won't be forever."

"Oh, I know it won't." The firm set of Nate's jaw answered that question. "Tori has a lot of faith in you. Don't let her down."

"I won't."

"So, did you ask her out?" Nate asked a bit too enthusiastically.

"What? No! I would never cross that line."

Nate stared at him for a second before realizing what he'd asked. "I'm not talking about my wife. Geez, what kind of man do you think I am? I meant Chelsea."

Of course he did. The woman he couldn't shake from his thoughts...or his dreams. Her denim blue eyes were forever ingrained in his soul. When he was around her, he'd never felt more lost—and found—in all his life. He just didn't know what had prompted Nate to ask about her.

"Where did that come from?"

"Our kitchen window faces the bunkhouse, so we

had a ringside seat. You two looked friendly, which surprised us after the fit she pitched over you working here. Come on, don't keep me in suspense. Did you ask her out or not?"

It had been bad enough Peyton had watched them from the car, let alone his ex-wife and her husband. "We talked about maybe getting something to eat, but Chelsea wants to run it by Tori first." Ryder's conversations with Nate were already awkward despite both of their best efforts. Discussing Tori's feelings about the possibility of her ex-husband dating her friend made it all that much worse. "She doesn't want to step on any toes."

"Why should Tori care?" Nate angled his horse to face Ryder. "You two divorced years ago. Clearly she's moved on. Besides, it's not like it was a real romance. You married for Missy's sake. That was an admirable thing to do and Tori will always be grateful."

Admirable? Grateful? Nate made it sound as if he'd been a figurehead and nothing more. They had been a family even though he and Tori had never been in love with each other. He held his tongue, not wanting to start a fight with the man who had the power to end his freedom with a single phone call.

Nate was marking his territory and Ryder had already decided he liked him better when he was on the road. The man may have agreed to let him live on the ranch, but that didn't mean he was happy about it. "I think it's the attorney in her. They always have to verify things."

"There's a barn dance at Schneiders Dance Hall tonight and Tori told me Chelsea will be there."

Yeah, because setting him up with someone else meant he wouldn't be interested in Tori. Maybe if he didn't respond, Nate would go away.

"You should get to know her better since you two will be spending more time around each other."

Now Nate had his attention. "What do you mean?"

"Chelsea volunteered to work here on the weekends, for a few hours at least. She claims not to know anything about horses, but Tori and I figured you could change that."

Ryder inwardly groaned. "Whose idea was that?" Attraction or not, he didn't want to mix business with pleasure. Not when his freedom depended on his job performance.

"Judd's, but she agreed."

"I bet." Tori's brother looked like he had just stepped out of an issue of *Men's Fitness*. She'd probably agreed to volunteer because of him.

"So, are you coming to the dance? Tori, Missy and I will be there."

Along with the rest of the town. He was still trying to warm up from his frosty reception at the Iron Horse Bar & Grill a few nights ago. "I'm not sure if the timing is right."

"The timing's perfect. You're single and Chelsea's single."

"I never took you for a matchmaker, Nate." Sadie shifted beneath him, sensing the tension in his body. "I meant Saddle Ridge isn't ready to accept me as an active member of society just yet."

"I don't know much about you outside of what Tori

has told me. But you don't seem like a man who lets other people dictate his life. No one else would have gone to jail and allowed their family and friends to ostracize them for a crime they didn't commit. That alone takes balls the size of Montana. This is the hand you chose to play. So play it. Go all in and live a little. Right now, you're using everyone else as an excuse not to."

Nate nudged his horse backward, then took off in a run down the hill. Since when had not wanting to upset anyone become an excuse? Under any other circumstances, he would have brushed off the whispers and stares. But he'd killed a man everyone had known and loved. At least they thought he had. That was what they needed to believe because the truth would destroy what remained of his severely fractured family.

He finished out the rest of the day without running into Tori or Nate again. The weekend volunteers made it easier for him to focus on taming wild horses to ready them for adoption than endure forced conversations with people who were either afraid of or angry with him. Tonight, he planned to swing by his uncle Jax's grave to pay his respects since he hadn't been able to attend the funeral last year. Afterward, he would head to the supermarket to grab a thick steak to throw on the grill. That was all it took to make him happy. He'd always been a simple man…just needed food, shelter and the company of a loyal friend or two. So what if it was Saturday night and Chelsea would be at Schneiders surrounded by eligible men?

Men without prison records.

Men without baggage.

Men that weren't him.

Who was he kidding? He was going to Schneiders.

Chelsea would have stayed home tonight if Missy hadn't already told Peyton about the barn dance. Jocelyn had mentioned earlier that she'd be there, too. Hopefully, she hadn't lined up available men for her to check out. *No thank you.* She still hadn't decided whether or not to go on a date with Ryder. If she could get Tori alone later, she'd talk to her about it. Maybe. A part of her wanted her friend to have a problem with Chelsea dating her ex-husband. The other part feared she wouldn't. And then what would happen? Would she really do it?

She hadn't dated since before Peyton was born and even then, Peyton's biological father hadn't exactly courted her. They'd had sex a few times, she'd gotten pregnant and that was that. Raising her daughter alone had left little time for socializing. Between finishing college, law school and working…and then moving to Saddle Ridge last year, she already had a jam-packed schedule. So why had she agreed to volunteer at Free Rein?

Because she needed her head examined. Her attraction to the cowboy had been the driving force behind it when her motivation should've been the animals and the animals alone. Thankfully she'd had the good sense to request what she assumed would be a Ryder-free job. That was one man she couldn't picture in an office pushing papers. He was raw and rugged and belonged outdoors.

Once again, her mind wandered where it shouldn't.

Chelsea stood in front of her bedroom's full-length mirror and stared at her reflection after changing for the tenth…or twentieth time. "This is crazy. I don't even know if he'll be there tonight." Chances were he wouldn't since he still had a lot of family to catch up with. "It's just a silly dance."

Her black rhinestone top, jeans and black cowboy boots would have to do. Plus, they made her look ten pounds thinner and after the way she'd been stress eating lately, she could use the help.

Downstairs, she hustled Peyton into the car and drove the couple miles to Schneiders Dance Hall. Behind the main building, they had a large timber-framed barn where they held weddings and parties in addition to the monthly concerts and all-ages welcome barn dances. She had attended a wedding there a few months ago and had been more impressed by the authentic post-and-beam construction than she had been by the event itself.

Peyton flattened her palm against the car window, feeling the vibrations of the music. They hadn't even finished parking and Chelsea could make out every word the band played. She reached for Peyton's hand as they got out, surprised by how many people were there. Crowded places made her nervous. It had been one thing when she'd been able to yell her daughter's name to get her attention. It was a whole other story now that she had to rely on Peyton seeing her first. She stood just shy of four feet tall and easily disappeared in a crowd.

Peyton bounced up and down in excitement as they

walked inside. Rows of line dancers boot-scooted and toe-stomped under strands of twinkling white lights that hung from the barn's exposed beams as couples twirled and two-stepped around them. Peyton spotted some of her friends from school and tugged her in their direction. At least she felt normal amongst the other kids. It had been three long years of adjustments and they still had a lot to learn. Chelsea was glad the children had one another to talk to tonight because she would bet money that ninety-nine percent of the people there had no way to communicate with her daughter unless they typed it out on their phone and showed it to her. It amazed her how long it took most people to recognize Peyton was deaf and not some kid screwing around. Yet educators continued to stress the importance of learning a second language like Spanish or French, but rarely mentioned sign language. It frosted her that few schools even offered it as an elective when approximately three kids out of every thousand were born with a discernible amount of hearing loss.

But Ryder knew. He had zero problems communicating with her daughter and that made him sexy on a whole other plane.

Tori tapped her and Peyton on the shoulder, drawing Chelsea out of her internal drool fest. "Come sit with us. Nate snagged a table."

The band played Miranda Lambert's "Kerosene" as Chelsea shimmied her way across the room—and apparently embarrassed Peyton judging by her eye-roll head-shake combo. She knew she looked like a duck on crack when she danced, but she didn't care. She hadn't danced in forever. She'd almost made it to the table when Jocelyn grabbed her by the waist and spun her onto the dance floor, causing her to lose her grip on Peyton. Tori signed she'd watch her and then took out her phone and began recording Chelsea's stellar moves as Jocelyn pulled her deeper into the crowd.

"I heard you and Hottie McHottie Ryder Slade had a little somethin-somethin going on outside the restaurant the other day."

"Good Lord." Chelsea covered her nose. "I hope you're not driving home. You need a breath mint and a cup of coffee."

"Don't you dare change the subject. Now I know why you kept swiping left." Jocelyn wrapped her arms around Chelsea's neck and rested her forehead against hers. "You have a thing for the cowboy."

"And you've had too much to drink." Chelsea attempted to look for backup, but Jocelyn refused to let her go. "Are you here alone or did you come with someone?" She hoped not with one of her online dates.

"My sister—Maddie—and her boyfriend. My date canceled shortly after we got here. Don't change the subject."

That explained the alcohol.

"I'm not. There's nothing to tell you about Ryder. We talked, and he left."

"Then how come I heard you were running your hands all over his chest?"

Chelsea swore the fumes emanating from Jocelyn were making her drunk.

"That's not what hap—"

"There you are." Maddie squeezed in between them, breaking Jocelyn's death grip. "Time to get you home." Her lips thinned as she attempted to smile. "I'm sorry, Chelsea. She's had a rough night."

"Do you need any help getting her to the car?" She tugged the hem of Jocelyn's shirt to keep it from riding up as Maddie draped her sister's arm around her shoulder for support.

"I got it. I think." She waved her boyfriend over. "Where's your date?"

"I came with my daughter."

"Oh, I thought Jocelyn said you were dating Ry—"

"She was mistaken." This was how rumors started in a small town. "Are you sure you've got her?"

"We're good. Have fun." Maddie half walked, half dragged Jocelyn toward the door.

"I will." Chelsea wondered if people would talk about Jocelyn's intoxication as much as they had discussed her and Ryder's fictional romance. Although after last night maybe there was a little truth in fiction. She made her way to the table, scanning the crowd for him as she went. After dealing with Jocelyn, she needed a stiff drink of her own. Instead, she'd have to settle for the round of Cokes Tori had ordered. After all, she was driving.

"What's wrong?" Tori asked.

"There seems to be a rumor going around that I'm dating Ryder."

"I think you two would be cute together."

"You do?" Chelsea had intended on having this conversation at some point, but she hadn't expected Tori to agree or at least agree so quick. "You'd be okay with that?"

"Look." Tori leaned toward Chelsea. "This isn't common knowledge, but Ryder and I had a special kind of marriage. He was and still is my best friend...just don't tell my husband that last part." She checked to make sure Nate was out of earshot before continuing. "I love Ryder, but we were never in love with each other. He took care of me and Missy when I had nobody else."

"It was a marriage of convenience?" She'd gotten a completely different vibe from Ryder the night before.

"Yes and no. Ryder loved Missy as his own. That part was real. The rest wasn't." She sipped her drink before continuing. "Ryder stood by me when Missy's sperm donor took off—" Chelsea smirked at the mention of Missy's biological father "—but a relationship like that can only go so far. We both deserved more, and I've found that with Nate. He's my happy-ever-after and I want Ryder to have the same thing. And if all you can offer is friendship, then that's fine, too. He could use that right now."

"I don't understand. He's from Saddle Ridge. Doesn't he have plenty of friends?"

"Not since his father's death." Tori's shoulders sagged. "I don't think most people will ever forgive him for what happened. And it wasn't—" Tori's eyes widened as if realizing she'd said too much. "Forget it."

"And it wasn't what?" Years in the courtroom had taught Chelsea when someone purposely left something out.

"I shouldn't even tell you this, but I want you to see

who he really is, because I think you would like that person." Tori twirled the straw in her soda. "Everyone in town loved Frank and Bernadine Slade, but behind closed doors…things were ugly. He and his brothers didn't have it easy growing up. There are five of them altogether, with only seven years between them. They were a handful, even on their best days."

"I can imagine." Chelsea had a hard enough time with one kid.

"They were a ranching family and money was always tight. They didn't go on vacations or spend a penny on anything that wasn't necessary. Harlan—he's the youngest—wanted no part of the business. And Frank wasn't thrilled when he joined the sheriff's department. Wes, who's a year older than Harlan, only had bull riding on his mind."

"So everything fell on the other three."

"No, it fell on Ryder alone. Dylan and Garrett, the oldest two, had already married. Dylan and his wife lived in Missoula and Garrett and his wife had already started a family and ranch of their own. Wes still lived at home, but he spent a good amount of time on the road competing. That left Ryder and his parents. When things went bad, Frank needed someone to blame."

"And Ryder was the target." She'd seen similar situations time and time again on the job.

"Exactly. I was there for Ryder just as much as he was there for me. I'd lost both my parents shortly after high school and had no one else to lean on for support. I needed help raising Missy and he needed out of that house. Our arrangement worked for years until I wanted more from life. When I look back now, I feel like I signed his death warrant by sending him away. He could have gotten a place of his own instead of moving home, but I think he always believed we'd work it out and that living with his parents was only temporary. I filed for divorce as fast as I could because I knew the sooner I cut him free, the better off he would be. Only that plan backfired."

"What do you mean?"

"Ryder had been served the divorce papers the morning of the accident. Unable to face anyone except a whiskey bottle, he spent the rest of the day at the bar. The bartender didn't know our marriage had ended and called me to pick him up. I got him out of there sometime in the middle of the afternoon and sobered him up a bit over coffee and a bite to eat at the diner. We talked for a while and then I drove him home that evening. That's when it happened." Tori's eyes brimmed with tears. "It was all my fault."

"No, it wasn't." Chelsea covered Tori's hands with her own. "You couldn't have known he'd react that way."

The other woman shook her head. "You don't understand."

"Then tell me." What was her friend hiding? "You can trust me."

Tori stiffened at her words. "There is nothing to trust you with. It's just the irony of the situation."

"How so?"

"Working on the Slade ranch meant Ryder was expected to put his paycheck right back into the business, that is when he got one. Frank made sure everyone else had their money before he paid him."

"I thought Ryder trained horses until his arrest."

"He did, and Frank battled him over it constantly. He felt since Ryder lived under his roof, he should work on the ranch and the ranch alone. But Ryder refused to abandon a horse in the middle of training. He did both jobs for a while, barely giving himself a chance to sleep. It caught up to him after a month or so and when he'd finished training a horse, he stopped taking on new ones, until eventually, he worked solely for Frank. He'd been adamant about paying me child support, but once he did he had nothing left."

"And by doing right by you and his dad, he didn't have the money to move out." Chelsea's heart broke. Not just because of the way his father had treated him but because of the way she had misjudged him. "I still don't understand. How is it ironic?"

"Because I'm doing almost the same thing to Ryder that Frank did. I can't pay him what he deserves so he can get a place of his own and I can't afford to let him go. The terms of his parole require him to work full-time and no one would hire him straight out of prison... at least not in Saddle Ridge. He's in the same vicious circle."

"Then why did he move back here?" Could he have real feelings for Tori? "The state has several programs for parolees."

"It's important for him to be near his brothers. Outside of Harlan, I can't see the other three talking to him anytime soon. They blame him for that night along with the rest of the town."

"What about his mother?"

"She sold the ranch, moved to California shortly after the funeral and remarried. She's never been back, not even for her sons' weddings or grandchildren's births and christenings."

And here Chelsea had thought Ryder had the support of his family when he only had Tori...and Nate.

The man caught her gaze as he approached the table. "Okay, you two, I've been waiting to dance with my wife since we got here."

An uneasiness fell over her as Nate smiled in her direction. "Go ahead, I'll watch the kids."

"The kids are fine. They're with their friends and some parents from school." Nate looked past Chelsea. "I have a suspicion you'll be out there dancing, too."

She took a deep, shaky breath as she turned around. Ryder, all six hunk-of-burning-love feet of him, strode across the crowded barn and stopped in front of her. "Ma'am." He removed his hat and winked. "May I have this dance?"

Chelsea looked to Tori. "Did you set this up?"

"No." She giggled. "But I think you should go for it."

"I think you should, too." Ryder reached for her hand and led her into the crowd before she could answer. "Do you know how to line dance?"

"Not very well." Chelsea hoped this didn't count as a date because she was about to make a fool out of herself. "If I break your toes, don't hold it against me."

"That bad, huh?" He laughed, wrapping his arm

around her waist and steering her to the perimeter of the dance floor. "How about we two-step for everyone's safety? I'll guide you through it."

Chelsea fought the urge to lean into his body. He could two-step her wherever he wanted at this point. "Don't say I didn't warn you."

"You'll be fine."

He slid his hand under her left arm and cupped her shoulder blade, allowing her to rest her fingers just above his biceps. *Good Lord!* It took every ounce of her strength not to give it a squeeze. He raised their other hands, leaving a little less than a foot between them. It felt like too much and not enough at the same time.

"Wow, you're tense." He shook her arm. "Relax. It's only a dance."

"Something I'm horrible at. I haven't had much of a chance to go out dancing since I had Peyton."

"I doubt you are horrible at anything." His rough palm pressed harder against hers, causing her to crave more of him. "Just follow the beat. Quick, quick, slow, slow. A quick step is one beat. Slow is two. You step back when I step forward and I'll handle the rest."

The band began playing Jon Pardi's "Head Over Boots" as Ryder twirled her under his arm. He could have been teaching her how to shovel manure and she'd still find it intoxicating. Between his musky aftershave and his slightly crooked grin that promised mischief and magic rolled in one, she was a goner.

After a few stumbles, they traveled smoothly around the dance floor. "You're a pretty good teacher," she said as she fell in step with his rhythm.

"That's only because you're a willing participant. Are you ready for some more serious moves?"

Chelsea swallowed hard, heat spreading from her toes to her fingertips. She knew what he meant, but the underlying sensuality of his question made her want to see more of his moves here *and* in private. "I'm all yours, cowboy."

"If only that were true." He spun her under his arm, preventing her from responding, then he ducked under hers before guiding her back to his arms.

Dizzy from the dance and her heightened awareness of the power he had over her body, she held on tight to him. Tighter than she had any man. Tighter than she knew she should. Cinderella had nothing on her tonight.

Chapter 5

Ryder should have stayed home. He'd asked Chelsea for an innocent line dance and ended up holding her while they two-stepped around the barn. Now the entire length of her body pressed against his as the band played Brett Young's "In Case You Didn't Know." He wanted to push her away and pull her closer at the same time. Sentiment had always escaped him…until tonight. He finally understood what people meant when they said they never wanted to let someone go. He could stay in this moment forever and never tire of it. Unfortunately, the band didn't feel the same way. The song ended, and Billy Ray Cyrus's "Achy Breaky Heart" began.

"Dance with me." Peyton squeezed in between them, stomping her feet to the beat.

"Sign when you speak, sweetheart," Chelsea gently corrected.

"Momma, please stop." Peyton's smile fell from her pretty cherub face. "Let me be me for one night."

"Honey, you need to learn."

Peyton folded her arms across her chest. "I am learning. But I need a break."

Chelsea lifted a brow at Ryder. Lines of frustration etched across her forehead. "Am I being unreasonable?" she asked without signing.

That was a loaded question if he'd ever heard one. He wanted to comfort Chelsea, but he sympathized with Peyton too. "I think she just wants you to dance with her." He signed as he spoke, so Peyton wouldn't think they were hiding anything from her.

"I want to dance with you, too." The little girl reached for both of their hands, ending any further conversation. Peyton looked up at him with eyes the same blue as her mother's. Eyes that touched a man's soul and made him vow to love and protect them forever. Although that was purely speculative on his part, because he had no intention of ever marrying again. Well, maybe not never. Just not while he was on parole. He needed at least the next three years to get his life together. Until then, he had nothing to offer anyone.

That didn't mean he couldn't have fun tonight. He reached for Chelsea's hand and gave it a squeeze he hoped reassured her she was doing an amazing parenting job. The three of them danced together through four songs and Peyton's ability to detect the changing beat blew his mind. Since Missy had been born deaf, she'd

never known what music sounded like. Peyton had, and
when certain songs played, she recognized them well
enough to sing along.

"You have a remarkable daughter," he said after Peyton ran off with one of her friends. Another slow song
began, and Ryder tugged her to him without asking. "I
see a lot of you in her."

"Thank you."

Chelsea's dark lashes shadowed her cheeks as she
lowered her head. He fought the urge to lift her chin to
him, knowing he'd be unable to refrain from kissing
her. Because what man wouldn't want to kiss a woman
like Chelsea Logan? Intelligent, beautiful, successful.
And a strong single mother on top of it.

"Is Peyton's father around?" For all Ryder knew, the
man could live across town.

"Oh, no." She shook her head violently. "He left the
minute he found out I was pregnant. I had to hire a private investigator to track him down, so I could get him
to relinquish his rights to Peyton. Let's just say he was
a lesson learned."

"You're doing a wonderful job raising her on your
own."

"Are you sure?" She met his gaze. "I think you
thought I was being too hard on Peyton earlier."

"Not at all. You want what's best for your daughter and there's nothing wrong with that." Ryder silently cursed himself for saying a word because now
her mouth was dangerously close to his. He was in the
exact tempestuous position he'd feared only moments
ago. Her lips, full and lush, had taunted and teased him

in his dreams. Whatever stirred deep within him went way beyond a passionate night in bed. He wanted all of Chelsea Logan, but she was off-limits. At least until he straightened out his life. And even though he'd already asked her out, a part of him wished he hadn't. He wanted her company—in more than one way—but a date or two couldn't turn into a relationship. He had nothing to offer her and until he did, they'd both have to settle for this, and only this. Ryder groaned.

"Are you all right?"

"What?" Had he groaned out loud? *Crap!* "I was just thinking of something I forgot to do today." *Like keep you at arm's length.* He needed to get his mind off her body before she became physically aware of his thoughts. "What does Peyton want to be when she grows up?"

"An equine veterinarian. She has ever since she could say *horsey*. Even after she lost her hearing, that dream still burns inside her."

"Good for her. I'm glad she doesn't see her deafness as an obstacle." Maybe Ryder needed to take a lesson or two from the pint-size Logan. Especially after Nate accused him of using his incarceration as an excuse not to live his life. He may have had Chelsea wrapped up in his arms for the past hour, but he hadn't been oblivious to the stares and whispers that followed them around the dance floor. People could talk about him all they wanted. He'd survive. Chelsea and Peyton's reputations worried him more. Every fiber of his being told him not to let her go, but he had to. Releasing her, he stepped back and nodded toward the bar. "I could use a drink. Can I get you something?"

"Just another Coke, thank you."

Ryder sensed a twinge of disappointment in her voice. But it didn't hold a candle to the ache he already felt in his heart. He should have stayed home instead of leading her on and torturing himself. "I'll meet you at the table."

By the time he reached the bar, his desire had turned to anger. How could he have left her in the middle of the dance floor…alone? He could have at least walked her to the table. Either prison had stripped him of his social graces or he'd become an idiot during his incarceration. Who was he kidding? Chelsea was way too good for him.

"This is a surprise," a man said from behind him.

Ryder turned to see his brother Wes, and his fiancée, Jade, standing there. "I hope it's not a bad one."

Jade stared up at Wes, waiting for him to respond. When he said nothing, she broke the silence between them and gave Ryder a hug. "It's good to see you."

"You, too." The last time he'd seen Jade, she'd still been in high school. "I heard I have triplet nieces. I'd love to meet them." Out of the corner of his eye, he watched Wes's fists clench and unclench repeatedly. "Or maybe it's too soon."

"I think it's a great idea." Jade entwined her fingers with Wes's. "Don't you, honey?"

"No." Wes released her hand and stepped in front of her, blocking her from Ryder's view. "I don't want you anywhere near my children."

"Come on, Wes. We need to talk. Not here, but sometime soon." Wes more than any of his brothers had understood the hell of living under the same roof as their parents. The constant war that had brewed between them had been the reason his brother had competed in any and every rodeo he'd qualified in. Frank and Bernadine's dysfunction had taught Ryder how not to behave in a marriage.

"Why did you come back to Saddle Ridge?" Wes asked.

"Because I wanted to be near my family." The silence surrounding them screamed louder than a freight train. When had the music stopped? Ryder looked from face to disapproving face of the former friends and neighbors he'd grown up with. He'd known they'd need time to adjust to his being home, but he hadn't expected the mob mentality as they gathered behind his brother.

He could hear Tori swear as she pushed her way through the crowd. "What the hell is wrong with you people?" She scolded them before stopping in front of Wes. A foot shorter than his brother, she could drop any man to his knees with her death glare. "How dare you start this in public." She jabbed the front of Wes's shirt. "And how dare you show your face tonight if you had a problem with Ryder showing up, too."

"Me?" Wes puffed his chest. "I have every right to be here."

"So does your brother." She took a step closer. "He served his time for the accidental death of your father. Do you hear me, Wes? Ac-ci-dent-al."

"Okay." Ryder squeezed between them. "That's

enough, Tori. I don't need you standing up for me. Wes can feel however he wants to feel ab—"

Ryder never saw the punch coming. Just shy of the sweet spot, his brother knocked him to the ground with one solid blow.

"Oh, my God!" Jade shouted. "Wes, what did you do?"

"It's all right." Ryder picked up his hat and rose to his feet. "He's wanted to do that for a long time. It doesn't make me love him any less." Despite Wes's own issues with their father, the man had still been their father, and his death had eliminated any chance of them ever reconciling their differences.

"Let's go." Jade yanked Wes's arm until he relented and followed her out of the barn.

"Give me a shot of whiskey." Nate smacked the bar top behind him.

"You're bleeding." Tori handed Ryder a wad of napkins. "He had no right to do that."

"Yeah, well, I'm not surprised."

"Hopefully he got it out of his system now." Nate handed him the shot. "Here, this is for you. You look like you could use it."

"Thanks, man." Ryder closed his eyes as he tossed back the amber liquid. The smooth smoky sweetness burned as it slid down his throat, briefly taking away the pain along his jaw. The band began to play as the crowd faded into the background once again. He set the glass on the bar and turned around to see Chelsea standing at the edge of the dance floor with Peyton, watching him.

Yep. He should've stayed home tonight.

* * *

Chelsea hated Mondays, especially when she still had Saturday night on the brain. It wasn't so much what had happened between Wes and Ryder, although it had frightened her when everyone at the dance stood behind the younger Slade. Or that her daughter had witnessed the spectacle and asked a million questions when they got home. None of which she could answer. It had been Tori and Nate's reactions. Tori had defended Ryder as if her life depended on it, and Nate had not only let her, he'd bought Ryder a drink afterward. She couldn't put her finger on why that had bothered her, but the situation felt off somehow. Especially after her conversation with Tori earlier that night.

Her office phone beeped, jarring her to the present. The screen displayed Stephen Jacobs's name, the senior partner who had warned her about Ryder the other day.

Chelsea pressed the intercom button. "Yes, Mr. Jacobs."

"Will you come to my office, please?"

She checked her watch. "I'm meeting with clients in a few minutes. Is it possible to wait until after they leave?"

"No, it's not."

Chelsea closed her eyes and sighed. "I'll be right there."

The walk between her office and Stephen's reminded her of a scene from a bad horror movie. The one where the buxom blonde walks down a long corridor and opens the closed door at the end, but the audience knows she's about to meet a violent death.

She gripped the knob, glancing over her shoulder one last time before turning it. And sure enough, half the firm had poked their heads out their doors to watch.

"Wonderful." She drew her shoulders back and pushed open the door. "Mr. Jacobs, you wanted to see me."

"Have a seat, Chelsea." He motioned to the leather chair across from his desk without even the courtesy of meeting her gaze.

She closed the door behind her and checked her watch again. Two minutes until her nine o'clock appointment arrived if they weren't in the lobby already. She'd never been one of those attorneys who made their clients wait. *Tardiness* and *rude* were synonymous in her book.

"The other day I spoke with you about Ryder Slade and how your relationship with him had been brought to my attention." Stephen leaned back in his chair and deadpan stared at her. "At that time, you told me there wasn't a relationship. This morning I was not only told otherwise, I saw a video of you and Mr. Slade dancing rather intimately Saturday night."

Chelsea's blood simmered beneath the surface of her skin as she fought to keep her annoyance under control. "With all due respect, who I date or don't date is none of this firm's business, and therefore, none of yours."

Stephen's head tilted ever so slightly at her rebuke but he remained expressionless. "No, but the contract you signed has a morals clause. As an employee, you are held to certain behavioral standards so as not to bring this firm into disrepute."

He can't be serious. "And I have adhered to those standards. Dancing with Ryder Slade in no way disgraces this firm."

"What about the incident that occurred?"

"The one where his brother approached and punched him with no provocation whatsoever? That incident?" Chelsea slid forward in her chair, perched on the edge and doing her damnedest not to storm out of his office. "Ryder Slade is on parole and free to go anywhere he wishes in this town. There are no restraining orders preventing him from doing so. The man accidentally killed his father, pled guilty, served his time and now he's out. Again, my friendship with Ryder is irrelevant."

"Let me ask you something, Chelsea." Stephen clasped his hands in front of him on his desk. "Say you're in the middle of a custody case and you're representing the father. What would you do to the mother on the stand if she was dating a parolee who had been convicted of killing his father?"

A bead of perspiration trickled down her spine. Stephen had purposely raised the heat in his office and had probably pocketed ice packs under his jacket. As a criminal attorney, he'd been known to use the tactic while deposing the other side.

"I would try to discredit her on the stand..."

"Exactly." He grinned in satisfaction.

"You didn't let me finish. I would try to discredit her on the stand if adequate proof existed that the man in question was a threat to her or her child. The sole fact he's an ex-convict won't hold up in court. Any judge will toss that argument."

"Any sworn judge. Our clients are their own judges and juries when it comes to these matters. You don't have to worry about your nine o'clock meeting." He reclined against the back of his chair. "They contacted me personally over the weekend. The Williamsons no longer feel comfortable with you as their attorney, or with us as their firm."

"They walked?" Chelsea's pulse drummed in her neck.

"They ran."

She didn't know what to say. What could she say? She refused to defend her actions any further. She didn't regret dancing with Ryder and she refused to allow anyone to condemn her for it. But in the same breath, she needed her job. She needed clients to trust her enough to believe in her abilities to represent them.

"Do you have anything to add?"

She lifted her chin, determined not to show fear. "Are you firing me?"

"No, you are too valuable of an asset to this firm." Stephen rose and came around to the front of his desk to stand before her. "But this can't happen again."

Chelsea stood, refusing to allow him to tower over her. In heels, she was almost an inch taller than him. "Are you referring to Ryder or losing clients?"

She hid a smile of satisfaction as she watched his Adam's apple bob when she used his own tactic against him.

"Well." He strode to the door, increasing the distance between them. "I would like to say both, but we know

I can't do that. My *recommendation* is to either keep your distance from Ryder Slade or improve his image."

She hated to agree with Stephen after his little power play, but maybe he was onto something. Ryder wanted nothing more than to make amends with his family. If they saw him in a different light, they might forgive him or at least begin to, and the rest of the town would follow suit.

"You may have just given me an idea. But I'll need your help."

Stephen's hand slid from the doorknob he was about to turn. She'd never seen him defeated or wary before. At least not of her. "With what?"

"I remember a client—this was shortly after I started working here—who ran an at-risk youth program on a ranch nearby."

"The Bloodworth Ranch in Whitefish. The owner's name is—let me think—Drew… Drew Kent. I represented a parolee that ended up working there. Is that what you want? For me to get Ryder a job there?"

"Yes and no. Ryder already has a job and they desperately need him. But, volunteering at an at-risk youth program would help rebuild his character."

"It might." Stephen rubbed his chin. "I must admit, I honestly figured you would've taken the easy way out and walked away from Ryder. Either there's something serious brewing between you two or you really believe in him."

"I believe in him." She didn't know why. In the back of her mind, it had something to do with Nate and Tori's reactions Saturday night. The three of them were hiding something, and she suspected the truth was more to Ryder's benefit, not his detriment.

Stephen returned to his desk and jotted down a note. "I'll give Drew a call and see what he says. I'll let you know."

"Thank you." A powerful relief filled her as she strode to the door and opened it. Her idea had potential especially if Stephen advocated for it alongside her. Somehow, she'd convince Saddle Ridge to give Ryder a second chance.

The Williamsons had done Chelsea a favor. She had planned to spend part of the afternoon drafting their wills, but since they were no longer her clients, she used that time to visit the Bloodworth Ranch. Despite Stephen's earlier antics, he remained true to his word and got in touch with Drew that morning. Since Ryder would be a volunteer, he had no qualms about his working there a few hours a week. That was if she convinced Tori to let him have the time off…with pay as part of a community project. She wasn't sure which would be harder…convincing Tori to spare Ryder for a few hours and take the tax write-off or talking Ryder into taking the job.

She pulled into Free Rein's parking area after picking up Peyton from school. That alone had been a rare luxury. She'd run into Tori while she waited for classes to let out and asked if she had time to chat today. Tori cautiously agreed, and Chelsea wondered if she thought she'd attack her again about Ryder. She hoped her generosity mirrored her relief when she heard why she was there.

"Mommy, look!" Peyton shouted much louder than she had probably intended, unaware of the intensity of her voice. After three years, it still caught Chelsea by surprise.

She followed her daughter's gaze to Ryder, who stood in the center of a round pen lunging a stunning black mustang. The majestic animal trotted in a circle around him as he held the lunge line in his left hand and a whip in the other. Peyton gasped when she saw him tap the horse's rump with the whip. "It's okay, sweetheart." Chelsea signed. "Ryder's not hurting him. He's correcting the horse's mistakes."

"But he looks perfect already."

From a distance he did, but she wasn't a horse trainer. "You know how Mommy used to sit behind you and guide your hand as you learned how to write your letters? Ryder's doing the same thing. He's guiding the horse."

Satisfied with her explanation, Peyton dragged her inside Tori's house, without so much as a knock. She beelined to the kitchen and climbed up on the stool at the breakfast bar where Tori had already set out a plate of peanut-butter-covered sliced apples. Chelsea set her handbag on the polished granite and watched her daughter happily tell Missy about a boy she had a crush on. Tori joined in, reminding them both they were too young for boys.

For the briefest of moments, Chelsea felt like an outsider in her daughter's life. She imagined this had been

Peyton's daily routine before she took it away. There wasn't anything wrong with her having a daily routine with Missy and Tori, she just hadn't been aware there was a routine outside of the one they shared.

"I hope you coming here today means you'll allow me to pick her up from school again."

Peyton watched her intently, waiting for her response.

"If you're okay with it, I am too," Chelsea signed.

"Thank you, Mommy!" Peyton hugged her with one arm while she munched on her apple slice with the other.

"She's welcome here anytime." Tori ruffled her hair. "I'm glad you changed your mind. After the other night, I wasn't sure."

Chelsea nodded toward the great room, and Tori took the hint. She wanted to discuss Ryder and the Bloodworth Ranch without prying eyes.

"Is Nate around?"

"He's on his way to Nevada to retrieve his trailer and pay off the transport fees on the mustangs he rescued."

"Is that one of them with Ryder?"

"Oh, no. They won't come near humans for a good while. We need to earn their trust after the way they've been treated." Tori tilted the thick wooden slats of the blinds overlooking the round pen. "That's Cactus. I named him that because he was a prickly thing when he first arrived. He's been here for two years and has the most potential."

"Will you put him up for adoption?"

"No." She returned her attention to Chelsea. "Don't

tell Ryder, but that's his horse. It doesn't make up for his mother selling Dante after his arrest, but Cactus took an instant liking to him when he arrived. They seem to understand each other."

Chelsea continued to watch Ryder through the window as she envisioned his muscles flexing beneath his tan flannel shirt. "Any idea who bought Dante?"

"I know exactly who bought him, but he's been unwilling to sell him back to me or Harlan. He's a good horse, and he doesn't feel Ryder deserves him. Harlan continues to try though."

"At least he doesn't feel the same way about Ryder that Wes does."

"If you had told me Wes would have reacted that way, I'd have said you were crazy. I'd like to believe Dylan and Garrett are better behaved than that, but now I'm not so sure. Ryder doesn't deserve the pariah treatment."

"That brings me to why I'm here. I think I have a way to begin changing people's minds about him. I hope you'll hear me out before you disagree."

Chelsea outlined the at-risk youth program and where Drew saw Ryder fitting in. "I don't want this to be a hardship for you, which is why I brought it to you first. If you can't afford to pay him, even with the tax write-off, I'll cover his salary for whatever hours he's not here. As long as you don't tell Ryder."

Tori shook her head. "Lying or hiding something from Ryder is never an option. He values honesty above all else. The truth always comes out and that might end any relationship you have with him, to say nothing of what it would do to my relationship with him."

Chelsea hadn't looked at it that way. "Fair enough."

"I like the idea of the program and I think he would do well working with at-risk children, but I doubt he'll do it."

"Why? This is a terrific opportunity for him."

"It is," Tori agreed. "But he's honor bound to Free Rein."

The nagging feeling that had taken up residence in the pit of her stomach reared its ugly head. "To Free Rein or to you?"

Tori's nostrils flared. "I am Free Rein."

Chelsea sat down at the chess table near the window to collect herself. Tori wasn't the enemy. There was no reason to give her the third degree. She lifted a translucent white pawn, rolling the cool onyx between her fingertips before setting it down two spaces forward. "You've told me how much you want him to succeed, so why don't you want him to volunteer at the Bloodworth Ranch?"

"I can't afford to let him work elsewhere and still pay him. A tax write-off only does me good at tax time." Tori joined her at the table, moving a black pawn of her own. "I need every dollar now for those animals. Your offer to cover his salary is generous, but he would never forgive either one of us, so I'd have to take the financial hit."

Chelsea moved her knight to a free space. "Not if I make a monthly donation to the sanctuary."

"I'm just going to come right out and ask." Tori moved her own knight. "If you're financially capable of doing that, why haven't you done so already? You're supposed to be my friend. You've been here every week-day to pick up your daughter for what…the last eight or nine months? You've seen how hard Nate and I struggle to keep the sanctuary running, but you've never volunteered your time or offered to sponsor one of our animals. Yet you have no problem volunteering when my brother asks or donating money for Ryder's sake. I'm sorry, but your offer comes across a little disingenuous to me."

Chelsea slid another pawn two spaces, and Tori immediately countered with her other knight. "You're a hundred percent right. I said the same things to myself the other day. I've been so laser-focused on my job and Peyton, I didn't see what you were going through." She toyed with the bishop before settling him next to her pawn. "That's why I volunteered. And that's why I told Judd I was embarrassed for not offering sooner. The same goes for the money. Regardless of whether or not Ryder volunteers at the Bloodworth Ranch, I will make a monthly donation to Free Rein starting today."

"Thank you." Tori moved her bishop next to Chelsea's. "Check."

"Crap, I didn't see that coming." She bumped her queen over two spaces.

"I can't risk losing Ryder to the Bloodworth Ranch." Tori claimed her pawn with a knight. "He runs a solid program. Ryder would make more money over there although he doesn't offer the parolees a place to live."

Chelsea nudged a pawn forward, poised to claim Tori's bishop. "Drew doesn't have room for another full-time parolee. I thought maybe you'd know that considering you were the one who told Ryder Free Rein was the only job available. I realize Whitefish isn't Saddle Ridge, but the 45-minute drive is nothing."

"Ryder wanted to be near his family." Sacrificing the bishop, Tori moved the pawn protecting her queen forward two.

"He still could have been." Chelsea removed the bishop from the table, which in turn caused Tori to claim hers. "Double crap!" She moved her queen back to its original position. "I know rents are higher in Whitefish, but he could have worked there and lived in your bunkhouse until he could afford to move."

"Why are we discussing this?" Tori's knight retreated. "You just said Drew doesn't have room for another full-time employee."

"No, but you knew about his parolee program and he would have hired him if there had been an opening." She slid her remaining bishop across the table.

"I needed him here." She nudged her queen one space. "He's the only one who would work for what I'm paying."

"The other day you said you felt guilty…is that why?" Chelsea jumped her knight. "You told me no one else would hire him. But how hard did you look?"

Tori shifted in her chair and pushed her queen forward, knocking one of Chelsea's pawns over. "I didn't look outside Saddle Ridge. Never said otherwise."

True, she hadn't, but for someone who'd said she'd felt incredibly guilty she couldn't pay him more, it baffled Chelsea that Tori hadn't expanded her search area or at the very least contacted the Bloodworth Ranch.

"Was it because you needed him here or because you wanted him here?" Chelsea claimed one queen with the other.

Tori blew out a long slow breath and studied the board. "Because he belongs here." Tori leaned forward and picked up her black horse. "Your inquisition is starting to tick me off, so I'll only explain this once." She struck Chelsea's queen and claimed the space.

"I'm not trying to imply that you and Ryder are together." Chelsea advanced her knight.

Tori's left eye twitched, setting her king on the run. "No, but I'm getting a definite vibe that you believe there's something going on here."

I'd bet money on it. Chelsea bumped her own king forward one. "Is there? Whatever it is, you can trust me. Heck, pay me a dollar and then you'll have attorney-client privilege."

"There's nothing to hide." Tori's black knight slid in front of her king.

Chelsea hadn't said there had been. "No?" She eliminated one onyx horse with another.

As if realizing what she'd said, Tori quickly continued. "Having Ryder work here means I can send him into town during the day and people will have a chance to interact with him. Maybe they'll even remember the person he was before this happened." Tori took out Chelsea's knight with the pawn she had planned to capture next. "I had hoped he'd run into his brothers and those chance meetings would help bridge the distance between them. After Saturday night I'm not so sure that's a good idea."

Chelsea positioned her rook, ready to end the game. "That fight made it all the way to one of the senior partners."

"What happened?" Tori blocked her with a pawn.

"Just a good dressing-down. He warned me about Ryder last week and again today."

Tori's eyes widened. "They can't tell you who you can date."

"No, but I was warned that any relationship with him would have consequences, starting with the clients I lost because they saw me dancing with Ryder." Chelsea overtook the pawn.

"I'm sorry." Tori sent another one forward. "I never imagined this would trickle down to you."

"I see bad things happen to good people all the time in the courtroom." Chelsea moved her rook forward another two squares. "Check. You'd think I'd be used to it. I may not know Ryder that well, but I can see something inherently good inside him. That's why I'd like to see him volunteer at the Bloodworth Ranch. Working for you is a great start, but that doesn't carry as much weight as him volunteering at a place he has absolutely zero connection to."

"Okay, but is there any way you can arrange for him to volunteer on the weekends and not during the week? At least then I have people here to help cover his absence." Tori moved her pawn, leaving her king wide open.

"I'll talk to Drew, but I think that's what he had in mind." Chelsea smiled, loving the taste of victory. "You just hung your king."

"What?" Tori stared at the table. "Did you call check?"

"Sure did." She nudged the black king off the board with her rook. "Your mind was clearly elsewhere."

"I guess so." Tori tugged the cord of the blinds and raised them, giving them a better view of Ryder. He had removed the lunge line from Cactus and stood in the center of the pen as the horse cautiously approached. He didn't reach for him or call his name. Instead, he remained quiet and still, allowing Cactus to decide if he wanted more from Ryder and not the other way around.

"Trust me when I say, you'll never find a better man."

Chelsea believed Tori, despite the nagging voice telling her there was more to his story. She trusted Ryder. If she'd been her own client, she'd warn herself the same way Stephen had. "Then help me convince him to volunteer at the Bloodworth Ranch."

"Okay." Tori wrung her hands. "You first. I need to check on our new horses. I'll take the girls in the truck. Let me know what he says."

"Before you go—" Chelsea ran into the kitchen and retrieved her bag from the breakfast bar. "Let me give you this first." She removed her checkbook and wrote out two amounts. "This one is my first monthly donation to the sanctuary." She handed the check to Tori.

"You just made a donation the other night."

"That was a special circumstance. This is what I promise to donate every month."

"Thank you." Tori folded the check in half and tucked it in her pocket as Chelsea finished writing out the second one.

"And this one is for babysitting Peyton every day."

"No, no, no." Tori walked away from her. "Absolutely not. Our kids are best friends. I refuse to make money off that. We discussed this the last time you offered to pay me."

"I don't care." Chelsea thrust the check at her. "Friendship aside, you're providing a service and deserve to get paid. I should have insisted months ago. You either take it or I'll find some other way to give you the money and you won't realize it came from me."

"Fine." Tori snatched it from her hands.

"Fine." Chelsea capped her pen and tossed it in her bag. "Friends?"

"Always." They both laughed. "Now go get your man. He's been sulking since Saturday night. I think he misses you."

"Yeah?" Chelsea slung her bag over her shoulder. "Then he should have returned my call yesterday."

"Uh-oh." Tori giggled. "You know how men are... stubborn as those donkeys out there, which you're now the proud sponsor of."

"I am?"

"I've been looking for a monthly sponsor for Jam Jam and Marmalade." Tori pointed to the pasture next to the round pen. "They're the smaller mother and daughter donkeys that are always together. I can't think of a better sponsor for them than you and Peyton."

"Jam Jam and Marmalade. I love that. They're perfect." She gave her friend a hug. "Thank you. Let's go tell Peyton."

"Nope." Tori spun her around and steered her to the back door of the great room. "You can tell her later."

She swung the door wide and gave her a little shove through it. "Go get your man."

"He's not my man." Chelsea tried to grip the door frame, but Tori pried her fingers loose. "I'm doing this to help rebuild his reputation."

"No, you're doing this so it will be socially acceptable for you to date him. And there's nothing wrong with that. Now go."

Tori was wrong. Half wrong, anyway. She really did want to see Ryder happy and accepted by his family along with the rest of Saddle Ridge. She also wanted to be the one standing next to him when it happened.

So what if it hadn't even been a week and she'd already put her reputation on the line for the cowboy? Her father always told her she had to "risk it to get the biscuit." She just prayed Ryder wasn't more of a gamble than she could handle.

Chapter 6

"Are you avoiding me?" Chelsea called from the fence rail.

"Not at all." Ryder had been painfully aware of Chelsea the moment her Impala turned off the main road. "Just giving you some space."

Cactus nudged his shirt pocket, determined to get the cookie Ryder had hidden there earlier.

"Funny, I don't remember asking you for it. If you're mad at me for leaving the dance without saying goodbye, I called Tori yesterday to get your number, so I could explain. I left you a voice message, but I never heard back."

"No explanation necessary. I understood why you left. Peyton should never have seen that fight. Missy shouldn't have either."

"That wasn't a fight. He cold-cocked you without provocation."

Ryder fished the cookie out of his pocket and gave it to Cactus. "My presence was enough to provoke him." The mustang nudged his shirt again as Ryder stroked his muzzle. "That's all the cookies I have." Cactus snorted, then walked away. It was progress. Each day the horse learned to trust him a little more. Eventually he'd win over his affection without the promise of food. After he completed training, Ryder would be hard-pressed to let him go. He'd make a great horse for whoever adopted him.

He opened the back gate of the round pen and released Cactus into the pasture to graze, needing the extra minute or two before he gave Chelsea his full attention. The push-pull war that raged inside him increased every time he saw her. He latched the gate and steeled his nerves as he turned around. There she stood, the low, late-afternoon sun silhouetting her features. Even though her eyes were in shadow, he still easily envisioned every fleck of blue and black within their depths. His boots grew heavier with each step. He hadn't counted on her watching him cross the sixty-foot sand-covered expanse that separated them. And it was crazy for him to think she wouldn't.

He gripped the top fence rail, his fingers inches from hers as he climbed over it until they were standing face-to-face. He tried his damnedest not to stare at the lush, full lips he'd been dying to kiss since they'd met, but it was too late. Chelsea needed to leave. To run and never waste another second thinking of him. Lifting his gaze to hers, he watched her pupils dilate with the sudden realization of his desire.

"You should go." Sending her away hurt almost as much as having her near. "I know you came here to talk about what happened, but I'm not going to. That's another reason I didn't return your call yesterday. Forget about the other night. All of it. I had no business asking you out or dancing with you. And don't blame Wes either."

"How can you brush off what your brother did?" Anger flashed in her eyes and a small part of Ryder reveled in the fact she felt the need to defend him.

"Because I should've visited my family before going out in public. I knew I might run into my brothers at the dance. I'm surprised it hasn't happened in town already. Thank God my nieces and nephews weren't there to see it. Your daughter should never have seen it either. I went there for purely selfish reasons and it bit me in the ass. Hard."

"What reasons?"

You. Only you. "It doesn't matter now."

"It matters to me."

"Why? You don't know me, Chelsea. This is what… the fifth time we've talked? We haven't gone out on a date, we haven't kissed, although Lord knows I've been tempted. But you and I can never be together. I have too much to straighten out in my life first."

Chelsea's brows rose as she stared at him. "You arrogant, self-righteous, son of—" She clenched her fists and stormed away from him, before stopping short and squaring off to face him once again. "How dare you think I'm hunting you down like a lovesick puppy. I came here to help you."

"I don't need your help."

"Really? Because the last I checked it wasn't normal for one sibling to go around punching the other... in public no less."

"You won't leave until I hear you out, will you?" Ryder hated the tone of the words coming out of his mouth, but Chelsea's anger was better than her love, or any remote form of it. "Fine, tell me what you think I need."

Her high-heeled foot tapped wildly on the ground and he wondered what she looked like stripped down... barefoot and barefaced, wearing only a plain T-shirt and an old pair of jeans. Made-up Chelsea excited him, but raw Chelsea intrigued him more.

"I don't know if I should even tell you now." She folded her arms across her chest.

"If you think I'm going to beg you, I hope you brought something warm to wear because we're in for a long, cold winter."

Chelsea's eyes narrowed, and for a brief second, she looked like she might spit nails. And then she smiled. "It won't work." She waggled her finger at him. "I see what you're trying to do."

Shit! He wanted to argue with her. He wanted her to run away and think the worst of him. But she wouldn't. She had more stick-to-itiveness than he'd given her credit for. "Fine, I'm listening."

"Have you ever heard of the Bloodworth Ranch?"

"No, can't say I have. Where are they located?"

"In Whitefish. The owner, Drew Kent, runs an at-risk youth program where they match parolees with troubled kids, so they can learn from not only their experiences but learn a trade as well. He could use someone to teach the kids the basics of horse training. The idea is to interest them in pursuing a career instead of looking for trouble."

"It sounds like a good opportunity for someone. But why are you telling me? I already have a job." Starting over in Whitefish might have been a possibility weeks ago. He'd still be close enough to visit family—well, Harlan—and he'd probably be able to walk around without people hating him. "I'm committed to Tori and Nate. I'm sure they are already taking heat for hiring me."

"That's why this is such a wonderful opportunity for you. Besides, his parolee program is already full. This is a volunteer position, a few hours a week and it will help rebuild your image, so to speak."

"My image?" Ryder didn't like the turn their conversation had taken. "How would that work? No one would know I was working or volunteering there."

"We would have to tell them. Tori, Nate, Harlan. Even me."

"It sounds like a PR stunt." One everyone would see through.

"A stunt usually benefits one party. This is a worthy cause. Those kids could use your expertise."

Maybe so, but the situation stunk of manipulation. "How did you find this program?"

"One of the senior partners at my firm represented a parolee there last year. I remembered the place and thought it would be a terrific way to show people you're giving back to society. My boss made a phone call, and I rode out there today and—"

"Whoa!" The realization why she had the sudden urge to help him hit him harder than his brother's punch. "This has nothing to do with me, does it? Your reputation took a hit the other night, and this is how you want to fix it."

She glared at him without a word. Could he have been any more of an ass? Instead of giving her the benefit of the doubt, he automatically assumed the worst.

"My reputation took a hit the day people saw you and me together in town."

Okay, he hadn't expected that. "Then why did you dance with me Saturday night? You should have told me, and I would've understood."

"Because I won't allow anyone to dictate who I can spend my time with. And before you get all riled up again...no, I didn't dance with you to be rebellious. I'm attracted to you and I want to get to know you better. Although, your attitude today might make me change my mind."

This was the exact reason why he shouldn't be in a relationship right now. He wasn't ready. Five and a half years in prison had changed him. It would change anyone. He didn't know how to act without reacting anymore. He'd had to compartmentalize every emotion to protect himself and he'd forgotten how to let anyone in.

"Maybe I'm overreacting...a little. You caught me off guard. Give me Drew's phone number, I'll call and see what he has to say. But I don't want you or anyone running around town talking about it. If people find out on their own that's fine. Shamelessly force-feeding it into the Saddle Ridge gossip mill is the last thing I want or need. I'll run it past Tori."

"She's already on board with it," she said matter-of-factly as if he should've already known.

And he would have if she hadn't gone behind his back. "How many people did you involve in this before discussing it with me?" A little help was one thing, this bordered on overstepping. "I appreciate the effort, but you should have consulted me first."

She opened her mouth to respond, then snapped it shut. He could tell she wanted to argue with him. It was painfully obvious. So was the truth. "I apologize. You're right, I just hate the way everyone looks at you."

"Do you? Or do you hate the way everyone looks at you when you're with me?"

"Both."

Ryder hadn't expected her to answer so fast. "Chelsea, I'm flattered you've taken the time to do this for me." Ryder didn't want to sound ungrateful, but he didn't want to be her pet project either. "I appreciate everything, but please don't do this again. I'm still trying to figure out why you're risking your reputation. You need to accept me for who I am now. Not who you want me to be tomorrow. Besides, you have a little improvement of your own to do."

"Excuse me? What is that supposed to mean?" Her foot tapped again.

Ryder cursed himself for not keeping that last part to himself. "You told me the other night you don't get out much. You need to make time. Forget the picture-perfect image you seem to compete with, and just be you."

"Where the hell do you get off? I have a child to raise on my own. I can't just hire any babysitter off the street, and even if I could, I wouldn't leave my daughter home like that."

"I'm not saying you should go out every night, Chelsea. There are other sitters besides Tori. I'm sure the school or other parents can provide you with a list. Besides, doesn't Peyton spend any time with her friends at sleepovers or the movies? Times when you're not with her."

"Yes, but I usually have work to catch up on," she mumbled.

"Your dedication is honorable, but I'd like to see you let your hair down." Just as much as he'd love to run his fingers through it. And bury his face in her—

"That makes me sound uptight." The foot stopped.

"I'm not saying you're uptight, but I don't think I've seen the real you." The little voice inside his head told Ryder to shut up. To stick with the original plan and keep her away from him. The pounding in his heart told him otherwise. "I want to see you cut loose and have fun."

"I thought that's what we did Saturday night." Chelsea crossed her arms, shielding herself from the words he couldn't manage to get right.

"We did, up to a point. I'd like to see more of that side of you."

"Are you asking me out again?"

Ryder wanted to say no. To tell her he was making

a generalized statement and she should go on a few dates, with anyone other than him. But the thought of her with another man—even if it was just on the dance floor—devastated him.

"I guess I am. But not in public." Ryder kicked at the dirt. "I realize that sounds horrible. You deserve to go out to a nice restaurant, not that I can afford one. You deserve to be with someone who can show you off and take you to all the places your friends go. I can't offer that. I can take you hiking and horseback riding, or to the movies in another town. You shouldn't risk being seen with me, though. And as much as I would love to include your daughter, I don't think she should be around me. She'll tell her friends and they'll tell their parents and one way or the other it will affect you both. When it comes down to it, I can't offer you anything."

"How about we start with friendship?" She took both of his hands in hers and gave them a gentle squeeze. "You're putting way too much pressure on yourself. I would like to tell you I don't care what other people think because in many ways I don't. But I do when it involves my daughter. Especially after the other night. That's why I want you to talk to Drew."

"Why do you care so much?" And for that matter why did he care what she thought of him? They were still strangers. They didn't owe each other anything.

"I haven't figured that out yet. When I do, you'll be the first to know."

"Is it wrong of me to want to kiss you?" Ryder hoped the question didn't scare her as much as the prospect of kissing her terrified him.

Chelsea glanced over her shoulder toward Tori's house, then up at him. "Only if it's wrong of me to want you to. But I don't think we should. Not here. Not when my daughter may be watching us from inside."

Ryder released her hands and stepped back. "You're absolutely right." At least she'd let him down gently.

"I'm in no hurry. We have plenty of time." She gnawed on her bottom lip as if she wanted to say more. "I'll text you Drew's information. I should get back to Peyton."

"Yeah, I still have a lot to do here before the sun sets." Ryder didn't know how to say goodbye. He knew he had to, but there was so much more he wanted to say. Chelsea was right. They were in no hurry. They had time. Plenty of time. "We'll talk soon."

"I look forward to it. Bye." She hesitated for a second before turning away.

Ryder wanted to watch her leave. Lord knows it was a gorgeous view. But if he did, he would chase after her. He willed himself to walk away without a second glance. And damned if it wasn't one of the hardest things he'd ever done. Chelsea Logan had not only gotten under his skin, she was slowly coursing through his veins toward his heart. Intoxicating and addictive, she left him wanting more every time they parted.

He was in trouble. Definite trouble.

It had been almost a week since Chelsea saw or even spoke with Ryder. Tori had told her he'd adjusted his schedule somewhat this past week so he could meet with Drew at the Bloodworth Ranch in the early evenings. That was great, but she would've preferred hearing the news from Ryder considering she'd set the whole thing up.

Chelsea grabbed the remote for the lamp in Peyton's bedroom and pressed the button repeatedly to get her attention. Today was their first day volunteering at the Free Rein Wild Horse and Donkey Sanctuary and she didn't want to be late. Getting Peyton up and out the door during the week was always difficult, but on weekends it was next to impossible. This being a Sunday, she'd have her work cut out for her to be on time.

Chelsea sat on the bottom step and slid on her tennis shoes. Tori had texted her last night with very specific instructions on what *she* should wear...not Peyton. Workout leggings, a tank top or sports bra, a fleece jacket and sneakers she didn't mind getting dirty. Why? All the times she'd seen Tori at the ranch, the woman had been in jeans and cowboy boots. Chelsea had never been a fan of leggings outside of the gym, and unfortunately for her backside, she hadn't seen the inside of a gym in quite some time. Tori hadn't mentioned a T-shirt and Chelsea figured they'd get the yellow shirts the rest of the volunteers wore. Nevertheless, she threw one on over her tank top. She also grabbed a pair of wool gloves from the mudroom and an extra jacket for both herself and Peyton to be on the safe side.

She'd hoped Tori would have put them together, but that didn't appear to be the case. The only thing Tori had told her was that Ryder wouldn't be there today, which may be a good thing considering she hadn't heard from him all week. Of course, she could've picked up the phone and called him, but that seemed desperate. Especially after he'd told her she needed some self-improvement. As angry as it had made her, she couldn't exactly disagree.

She didn't mind accepting babysitting help from Tori or her parents for those few hours after school until her workday finished each day, but it bothered her to dump Peyton off on someone else just so she could have downtime. She envied the mothers who maintained an active social life while raising their kids. And she equally criticized them. When it came to her clients, she preached the benefits of a balanced life and never let them feel guilty for taking time for themselves. Yet she hadn't found that balance for herself. She took pride in being a hands-on mom. Probably too much because lately, she missed adult companionship. Sure, she had some kid-free moments outside of work, but nothing had compared to dancing with Ryder the other night.

Peyton stomped down the stairs, tearing the picture of him from Chelsea's thoughts. "Mommy, it's too early."

Chelsea didn't bother reprimanding her for not signing. It *was* too early. When she had volunteered, she'd figured on something in the afternoon. Not seven o'clock in the morning.

"I know it is, sweetheart. But don't you want to see Jam Jam and Marmalade?"

"I see them every day." Peyton rolled her eyes.

Chelsea would rather argue a case in court than try to reason with a nine-year-old. "Look at it this way…

every day you work with the animals is one day closer to becoming a veterinarian. Think of it like an internship."

Peyton appeared to consider her statement before shrugging. "I guess."

"I hate to break it to you, but if you want to become an equine vet, you better do more than guess. A job like that involves a lot of on-call work. You'll be on the road all hours of the day and night. Not just when you want to." Some people would argue that Chelsea placed too much stress on Peyton developing a strong work ethic at this age, but it had been something her father had instilled in her since she could walk. Her daughter had more obstacles to overcome than the typical veterinarian school-bound kid. Especially when she would have to focus on her interpreter during labs and presentations.

"Fine." Peyton trudged out to the car and slammed the door closed.

And some days her daughter was a typical child, complete with attitude.

They drove to the ranch in silence. Chelsea hadn't known what to expect today, but she hadn't expected to see so many people already there. In the rearview mirror, she saw Peyton sit up straighter in the back seat as they parked. "Are they all volunteers too?"

Chelsea twisted to face her, looking forward to the day her daughter was tall enough to ride up front, so they could talk easier in the car. "Yes. Anyone in a yellow shirt is a volunteer. You've seen a few of them when Mrs. James needed help during the week."

"Do I get a T-shirt too?" Peyton asked as they got out of the car. "The donkey on them looks like Jam Jam."

"Maybe if you ask Mrs. James nicely, she'll let you have one. I'm not sure where I'll be today, so do whatever you're told. Okay?"

Peyton stared at her. "You mean just like every day when I'm here and you're not."

"Lose the attitude, please. This isn't like every other day. There are more people around. People who don't know sign language. You stay alert and with Mrs. James."

Chelsea's nerves kicked in. Peyton needed to spend more time outside of the deaf community but that didn't mean Chelsea was ready for it.

Nor was she ready to see Ryder leaning against Nate's Jeep…waiting. For who? Her? He was supposed to be at the Bloodworth Ranch.

"I have such an exciting day planned for us." Tori ran up to them and gave Peyton a hug. "You girls are coming with me on prospective adoptee home inspections."

"They are?" Chelsea asked, not sure how she felt about Tori taking her child to strangers' houses.

Tori looked up. "I'm sorry, I should've asked you first since I'm taking them off the ranch. When I say homes, I don't mean actual houses. We'll be visiting a few ranches and making sure they're suitable for the rescues."

"It's fine." Chelsea swallowed down her apprehension. "You remember what I said earlier. You do everything Mrs. James tells you."

"I will. Bye, Mom." Peyton gave her a half hug goodbye and signed with Missy.

"I remember when she never wanted to let go. Now I'm the one with the separation anxiety."

"If you rather I don't take them today, I can have Nate do the inspections."

"No, it's fine. It will be good for her to see other ranches." Chelsea glanced over at the Jeep. Yep, Ryder was still there. "I thought he was working at the Bloodworth Ranch on weekends."

"Just on Wednesday afternoons and Saturday mornings. They worked out a schedule that doesn't interfere much with his work here. Makes me feel kind of guilty for biting your head off about it last week."

"It's all good. What am I doing today since you gave me such a specific wardrobe to wear?"

"Oh, those instructions didn't come from me. Ryder sent you that message."

"Why does he care what I wear?"

"Because you'll be with him all day." Tori beamed.

Chelsea's mouth went dry as her hands began to sweat. "And what exactly are Ryder and I doing today?"

"You'll have to ask him." Tori wrapped her arms around both girls' shoulders and ushered them toward her truck. "Have fun."

Chelsea made a mental note to strangle Tori this evening. Because whatever Ryder had planned she wasn't prepared for it. She forced herself to face the man waiting for her. She didn't know how she'd missed it earlier, but he wasn't wearing his trademark cowboy hat. Instead he had on a navy blue Free Rein ball cap. And instead of jeans, he had on jet-black running pants that emphasized the corded muscles in his thighs and calves. She had no idea beneath his jeans there were legs built like a racehorse. And she couldn't help but wonder what else on him was built like a racehorse. She cleared her throat as her eyes traveled up his body...to his fleece jacket. She didn't want to see fleece. She wanted to see a six-pack and arms of steel. Now that she knew what the legs looked like, she needed to see more.

Ryder followed her eyes. "I'm sorry, don't I meet your approval?"

"Since when do you need anyone's approval?" She fought to keep her eyes above his waist.

"Since your frown rivals the Gateway Arch in St. Louis? I know this isn't the most flattering outfit, but it's appropriate for where we're going."

"Not that you deserve the ego boost for this little machination this morning, but let's just say running pants do your body good. Now if you don't mind, I'd like to know what this is all about."

"It's a surprise." Ryder opened the Jeep's passenger door.

"Where are we going?" She'd never been a fan of surprises. Maybe that was the attorney in her. She always had to be prepared for the unexpected. Which apparently was all the time with Ryder. Not knowing what came next unsettled her...just as much as it excited her. And Ryder definitely excited her.

"If I told you, it wouldn't be a surprise. Do you trust me?"

She wanted nothing more than to trust the cowboy, but he wasn't making it easy.

"You know what, I'm a fool. Here I am, weeks out of prison and I'm asking you to trust me." He shook his head and removed his ball cap. "I was so excited about planning this today I didn't take into consideration how any of this might look. I'm taking you whitewater rafting. That is if you want to go."

"Whitewater rafting?" The words terrified her. "Isn't it too late in the season?"

"I ran into an old buddy of mine the other day. One of the few who doesn't hate me. He runs a rafting adventure place up in Glacier National Park and he told me this was the last day they were open for the season. He offered me free passes, and I thought it would be something great to do without worrying about who we might run into. I guess I should have asked if you're an outdoor adventure type of girl first."

"I don't know if I'm an outdoor adventure type of girl, considering I've done nothing remotely like this."

"Does that mean you won't go?"

"I'm not saying that. I'm just saying you may need to buy a pair of earplugs on the way there because I may scream in your ear during the entire rafting trip."

Chelsea had no idea what she'd agreed to or why she'd agreed to it. But she trusted Ryder enough to do it with him. She reached up and gave him a quick kiss on the cheek. "This is a sweet surprise. But I'll reserve my thank-you for the trip home when I know for sure I've survived this little river trek."

A soft tinge of red flooded his cheeks and Chelsea couldn't help giggling that she made a grown man blush. She climbed in the Jeep and in true gentleman style, he closed her door and climbed in beside her. The man had manners, she'd give him that. And now that they were truly alone, maybe she could find out what he, Tori and

Nate were hiding. Because no matter how many times she'd run through her conversation with Tori about the night Frank Slade died, her gut told her more had happened and only the three of them knew about it.

"Do you mind if I ask you something about your father's death?" Chelsea asked once they were on the road.

Ryder's knuckles turned white and the side of his jaw pulsated at the question. "If you must."

"Tori mentioned your relationship with your father and…" Chelsea fought the urge to drill him like a witness on the stand. The man wasn't on trial and she had zero proof that anything other than what Tori and Ryder said had happened actually happened. "She always seems to stop herself from saying too much."

"That's because she *is* saying too much." Ryder's tone had lost all its sexiness from only moments ago. "My father and that night shouldn't even be a topic of conversation."

"Unfortunately, it's not that simple to avoid."

"Yeah, it is." Ryder stopped hard at a red light and looked at her. "It's as simple as you just don't do it. It's my business."

"I realize that." Chelsea did. But she also knew from her job that hiding the truth rarely did any good, and he'd be better off not doing so. She also felt that, if they planned to be friends and he wanted to accept Chelsea's help—which he already had by taking the volunteer job—then he should trust her with this subject. "It's unavoidable when it comes up at work. Or when I have to check with your boss to see if you're available to volunteer at a parolee program. That night becomes a part of the conversation. And nice deflection by the way."

"What are you talking about?" Ryder shifted into first as the light changed. "Is this how today is going to be? Because if it is, I'm having second thoughts."

Chelsea sat in silence, fully expecting him to turn around and head back to Free Rein. He continued driving and after a few minutes, she saw the color return to his hands. But his jaw still pulsated and she heard the faint sound of grinding. She hadn't meant to make him mad, but his reaction only confirmed there was more to that night. And one way or another, she'd discover the truth.

But not today. She'd already blown her chance. And he didn't deserve an inquisition after planning their excursion. "I'm sorry. I wouldn't ask if I didn't care."

"I know. Your involvement with me puts your reputation at risk. That's why I wanted to do this today. To see how we are together away from everyone else. Where we can be ourselves without worrying what prying eyes might think or say."

"That's not the only reason why I care, Ryder."

"It's a big reason. Please don't deny it. You don't know me well enough to be invested in my well-being beyond human decency. You're worried about how people perceive you once they find out we're dating."

"Are we dating?" Because it sure felt like it fifteen minutes ago.

"No."

Well, that hadn't been the answer she'd expected. "Okay, then. Good to know."

"We're exploring. I don't think either one of us is ready to date."

No, of course they weren't. Eleven days ago, she hadn't even known he'd existed. Not that she'd been counting the days. Okay, so maybe she had. It still didn't make his declaration hurt any less. They were exploring. She didn't have the nerve to ask if he meant exploring the possibility of a relationship or exploring the river. Did it really matter at this point? He'd planned a fun adventure and she was ruining it by giving him the third degree.

"You're absolutely right." She squared her shoulders and began mentally preparing for the whitewater terror in her future. "So tell me, just how wet should I expect to get today?"

Ryder looked at her, almost swerving off the road in the process. "Sweetheart, don't ever ask a man that question."

"What?" Chelsea replayed the words in her mind. "Oh no, I didn't mean that." She buried her face in her hands as Ryder's laughter filled the Jeep's interior. At least she'd managed to change the subject…at her own expense.

An hour later, they pulled into a gravel parking lot in front of a massive log cabin. Once they filled out their paperwork and signed the foreboding risk forms, their guide led them to the wetsuit area.

"Can't we go as we are?" What was the point of Ryder telling her what to wear if she wasn't going to wear it?

"The air and water temperatures are too low today," the guide said. "You'll be much warmer in these."

A little part of Chelsea died inside when she stepped into the skintight abomination. Wetsuits were not meant for women who had a little extra going on. There was nothing like trying to impress a man when he could see every single one of her curves. And she had a few more curves than most women.

"You could've warned me about the wetsuit." Chelsea tried to swallow her bitterness.

"Number one, I didn't know about it. And number two, if I had would you still have come?" he asked as he zipped up his suit.

How was he already in the blasted thing when she couldn't get hers past her Lycra-covered thighs?

"Maybe. After going on a crash diet." She tugged hard, causing her hand to slip off the wetsuit and almost knock herself out in the process. She was hot and out of breath and they hadn't even begun their little adventure yet.

"Do you need a larger size?" the guide asked.

Really? Could this get any more embarrassing?

"Yes, please."

"You don't need a crash diet." He held the legs of the wetsuit as she peeled her calves from it. "I love every inch of your body. I have since the moment I met you." He rose before her and lifted her chin. "I mean that with all that I am."

Kiss me, kiss me, kiss me. This was the Ryder she wanted to explore today.

"Try this one." The guide nudged her arm with another wetsuit, breaking the moment. Ryder stepped back and gave Chelsea space.

The second wetsuit glided over her leggings with little effort and she didn't know if she should be flattered that the guide thought she was three sizes smaller or if she should kill him for embarrassing her.

"Are you ready to do this?" Ryder took her neoprene-gloved hand in hers.

She exhaled the breath she'd been holding. "Let's do it."

Chapter 7

"That was amazing!" Chelsea squealed as she climbed out of the raft. "I've never been more terrified and excited at the same time."

"I'm glad you enjoyed it." He resisted the urge to pull her into a kiss, their earlier argument still churning in his brain. But that didn't mean he wasn't tempted. Chelsea's usually perfectly styled hair hung wet and wild over her shoulders. Any makeup she'd worn had washed off in the river. This was the woman he'd been dying to see. Why couldn't it always be like this? No pretense. No history. Just living in the moment. "I've never seen anyone as happy as you are right now." He wanted to say *and more beautiful*, but he didn't want her to become self-conscious like she'd been earlier. Not that she had any reason to be.

"I thought I would hate this. You took me way out of my comfort zone, I didn't know whether to laugh or cry when you told me where we were going."

Ryder tugged off one of his neoprene gloves and tucked a strand of wet hair behind her ear. "And now?"

"Blissfully happy." She stepped toward him and snaked her arms around his neck. "This was just what I needed." Her eyes fluttered closed for a second before meeting his again. "Thank you."

"You're welcome." His mouth hovered inches above hers. He wanted to, needed to kiss her. To taste her. But he couldn't. Not until he was sure she'd leave his past in the past. "Maybe we can go on some other outings this winter."

"This winter, huh? It's nice to know you're still considering going out—I mean exploring—with me in the future."

Hell, right now Ryder had a hard time thinking of anything other than the full length of her body pressed against his, and if he didn't put some distance between them, the rest of their rafting group would soon be aware of his attraction to Chelsea. The second group paddled to the shore, giving him reason to break from her grasp. "I'm going to help them get our raft out of the water."

"Okay." The slight pout of her lips only confirmed she'd wanted to kiss him as much as he wanted to kiss her. He knew he'd regret it tonight, when he lay in bed… alone. He only prayed Chelsea would take precedence in his dreams tonight instead of the nightmares he'd been having the last few nights about the accident. He'd gotten to where he wouldn't go to bed until he'd exhausted himself to the point of breaking. And even then, random images of Tori and his parents haunted him.

Ryder waded into the river. The temperature drop forced him back to the present. His wetsuit offered protection from the frigid glacial waters, but he wouldn't want to stand in it for too long. If only he could wrap a wetsuit around his heart to protect him from the woman watching him from the rocky beach. She'd gotten under his skin in one too many ways.

Once they loaded the rafts onto the trailer, they climbed into the van and rode back to the rafting company.

"Would you believe this is my first time in Glacier National Park?" Chelsea grinned out the window. "Peyton's visited with school, but I haven't had a chance to see it myself. No photo could ever do this place justice. You were right. I need to make more time to do things like this. Maybe we can take her rafting this summer."

While Ryder loved that Chelsea had included him, he didn't want to make any promises he couldn't keep. "We'll see what happens. Maybe I won't be so much of a pariah by then."

She gave his hand a gentle squeeze and he fought the urge to entwine his fingers with hers.

"You need to reach out to your family. Ignoring your brothers and hoping they'll come to you solves nothing. Although I would caution you to stay away from Wes, or at least wear a helmet the next time you see him."

"Oh, you're funny." Ryder still felt the force of that

punch almost a week later. "I plan on talking to Harlan about that today."

"Have you seen him again?"

"No. He's been working the late shift and I've been getting my bearings at the Bloodworth Ranch in my spare time." A place he'd begun to feel guilty about because if a permanent position became available, he'd be hard-pressed to pass it up. He loved Tori for giving him a job when no one else in town would, but he wished he'd explored other options before agreeing to her offer. Even though she said she needed him, he was just as much of a burden to her and probably a thorn in Nate's side. Regardless of his generosity, no man was that confident. "Harlan's meeting me in Kalispell later this afternoon so we can talk privately since Ivy and Belle are at the house." Ryder never thought he'd need to meet his brother in another town, but after last weekend, he hadn't wanted to risk another public scuffle.

"I'm not trying to pry, but you never mention your mom. Do you ever talk to her?"

"No. Not since the night of the accident." And he doubted she remembered the conversation. He'd seen his mother drunk before, but never to that extent. "She lives in California with her new husband. From what I understand he has a huge family, and she's very involved in his kids' lives. I'm glad she's found happiness out there." Because she'd never found it in Saddle Ridge.

"What about her family here? She has grandkids."

"I'm not sure when she last saw Harlan's oldest daughter or Garrett's two kids. They may have flown out there to see her at some point. Harlan visited me in—" Ryder cut his sentence short, not wanting to divulge his past to the new acquaintances they'd made today. "Harlan only visited me a couple times a year. We didn't get much of a chance to talk about who went where." Instead, his brother had wasted their time together trying to discover what had really happened the night their father died.

"Only a couple times a year? I got the impression you two were closer than that."

"We are. It was too far of a drive for him to pop in. Plus, until last year, he was a single dad raising Ivy on his own. I wish I could've been there for his wedding. Dylan's and Garrett's too. I still can't believe three of my brothers got married within months of each other. And now Wes is engaged. I'm sure I'll miss that one too."

"When are they getting married?"

"I have no idea. I'm not privy to that information. It's better I don't know because I might be tempted to show up. Not to ruin it, but to wish them luck. I miss my family." More than words could ever say. "It looks like we're here."

The van rolled to a stop in front of the rafting company. It was almost three in the afternoon. Ryder had just enough time to get them back to the ranch and change before meeting his brother for dinner.

He helped Chelsea down from the van. A part of him already regretted ending their day early, but it was the only night that had worked for him and Harlan. The other part needed the reprieve. Between Chelsea's inquisition earlier and her exuberant thank-you on the riverbank, his frustration had reached an all-time high. "I have to ask. Have you swiped right on anyone lately?"

"I deleted my profile and the app. I was a fool for letting Jocelyn talk me into it. I don't have a lot of time to date." One of her brows raised as she looked up at him. "Why do you ask?"

"I was concerned about your safety." That and he didn't want to think about her body pressed against another man.

"As long as that's the only reason." Chelsea reached up and held his face in her hands. "I wouldn't want you to be jealous or anything." Rising on her tiptoes, she kissed him softly on the lips, her mouth lingering a second before backing away.

Ryder gripped her hips and held her in place. "Chelsea Logan, you're going to be the death of me."

By the time Ryder arrived at the bar and grill in Kalispell that evening, his stomach was protesting the lack of food. The rafting company had provided a picnic lunch along the river, but it hadn't been enough to satisfy his voracious appetite. His mother had always said he could out-eat ten men.

He tried not to think about her much. She had moved on and found the life she deserved. Hopefully she was sober. Tori had gotten her into one of the best and most discreet rehab facilities available. The recovery program had been why she sold the ranch so quickly. Not for the money. Her health insurance covered that. But to leave behind the painful past she had tried so desperately to escape in the bottom of a bottle.

Ryder pulled the parking brake on the Jeep and grabbed the keys. He appreciated Nate loaning him the vehicle until he could afford one of his own. The man may try to assert his dominance whenever he was home, but he had a good heart.

Harlan's police SUV pulled in beside him. "I guess I don't have to worry about anyone bothering us tonight." Ryder gave his brother a slap on the back bro-hug. "I hope you didn't wear your uniform for my benefit," he asked as they entered the restaurant.

"My shift just ended, and I didn't feel like driving home to change."

Ryder wasn't about to argue with him. If his little brother felt the need to protect him, then so be it. "How have you been? Are you getting any more sleep these days with the new baby in the house?"

They grabbed a booth and Harlan ordered an iced tea while Ryder ordered a beer under his brother's watchful eye. He'd forgotten what it was like going out with him. Always on duty, even when he wasn't. That was what made him a great deputy sheriff.

Harlan shook his head. "I don't remember Ivy being this difficult at almost six months old. At two months she had slept through the night. Occasionally she'd wake up and want to be changed or fed, but she was pretty good early on. But Travis…" Harlan raked his hand down his face. "It's every night. His diaper isn't wet. He doesn't seem to be hungry. All he wants is for Belle or me to hold him. And rock him. All night long."

"You know you're not supposed to give in to them." Not that Ryder was an expert on children. Missy had been an exceptional baby. She hadn't made a sound. Which he'd found unusual. Just because she couldn't hear didn't mean she couldn't cry or screech like other infants. But she hadn't. On the rare occasion she had, it had been more of a muffled whimper.

"We've tried to let him cry himself back to sleep, but one of us ends up caving. It's not just us who he keeps awake. Ivy has to get up and go to school in the morning. I can't send a half-awake kid to class." The waitress set their drinks between them. "You'll see. One of these days you'll have another kid."

"Don't be so sure about that." After witnessing their parents' dysfunction, he'd never been a big fan of the traditional marriage. That had been one reason he'd married Tori. They had a pressure-free marriage and came and went whenever they wanted. No, it hadn't been wine and roses, but they'd had companionship and mutual respect for each other. They'd never fought. Not once. And when Tori had wanted to go out, he'd been fine staying home with Missy. She'd become his little buddy and losing her had been no different than if she'd been his biological child.

"Dare I ask how it's going with Chelsea? I heard you went to the dance with her last week."

"We didn't go together." Ryder felt the inexplicable need to correct him. He didn't want the rumor getting out that they were spending time together. He didn't just want to protect her and Peyton's reputations, he wanted to protect the relationship. Which was ironic considering he didn't want to get involved with anyone. Yet he couldn't stop picturing a future with Chelsea. One he doubted would happen thanks to his past. "We ran into each other there and we had a good time until Wes's fist ran into my face."

"About that…" Harlan paused when the waitress approached their table and took their order. "I spoke with Dylan and Garrett. They'd like to see you."

Ryder almost choked on his beer. "Oh, really? I've been home for a couple weeks and I haven't heard a word from either one of them. I expected to run into them in town since Tori makes a point of sending me there for stupid crap every day. I can only assume it's because she's trying to force the issue. I've wondered if they are avoiding town to avoid me."

"They have been."

Ryder smacked the table. "Then why do they want to see me?"

"They're not avoiding you to avoid you. They are avoiding you because they don't want a public spectacle. After what happened with you and Wes at the dance last weekend, you have to agree with their reasoning."

Ryder sagged against the back of the booth. "Wes's punch, as shocking as it was, didn't surprise me. I wouldn't expect Dylan and Garrett to react to seeing me so violently."

"They wouldn't. They just don't want to run into you in town. Not for nothing, you could've called them once you were settled."

"I considered it. But unlike Tori, I didn't want to force the issue."

"And neither did they. That's why they're circumventing town for the time being." Harlan huffed. "All four of you are the most hardheaded men I've ever dealt with and I've dealt with more than my share of—never mind. I'll be glad when everyone's finally talking again so I don't have to be the mediator. Here's the bottom line." Harlan jabbed at the tabletop. "They want to see you, I know you want to see them, and if you're uncomfortable getting together at Silver Bells, then everyone can come to my house and Belle will take the kids somewhere so we can be alone."

The Silver Bells Ranch had belonged to Dylan and his uncle Jax before Jax had died last December. Garrett had moved back to town in January and signed on as his new partner. Wes had joined them earlier this month.

"I prefer not to do it at Silver Bells. That's Wes's home. I don't want to chance another blowup in front of his kids or Dylan and Garrett's. Your place is good."

"Fine. I'll set it up and expect you to be there."

"Anytime in the evening during the week works, except for Wednesdays." Ryder wanted to keep as much of his weekends free as possible. For Chelsea.

"How is that at-risk youth program?"

"From what I've seen so far, I love it. I love the whole Bloodworth Ranch setup. Drew has twenty parolees working for him. Men and women. They don't live on-site, but they work multiple shifts around the clock. It's a small cattle operation, but he also has crops and a ton of other livestock. The parolees learn all aspects of ranching and farming while they're there. They're only allowed to work there while they're on parole, then they move on to real ranching jobs."

"Sounds interesting. Why is this man so invested in parolees?"

"Because he was a parolee himself once. When he got out, he had a hard time finding work. I wouldn't mind setting up something like that of my own one day." If he could ever earn enough money to buy his own land. By the time he got off parole he'd be thirty-five. He'd hoped to have gotten a lot further in life by that age. He didn't believe in hocus-pocus or fairy tales, but this was one time he wished he had a crystal ball so he could see into the future and find out if he'd ever have anything worth offering Chelsea. "Once I've been there for a while, I want to sit down with Drew and find out how he started that business."

"I know this has been tough on you, but I have to ask…when are you going to tell me what really happened the night Dad died? Because we both know you weren't the one behind the wheel. That leaves only two people. Mom and Tori. Which one of them have you been covering for all these years?"

It wasn't even seven o'clock at night and Chelsea had already taken a long candlelit bath, drunk two glasses of wine and eaten a pathetic microwavable dinner. Missy had invited Peyton for a sleepover since they didn't have school tomorrow because of a teacher's conference. That gave Chelsea twenty-six kid-free hours. She'd already burned through four of them and now boredom had set in.

She could call Jocelyn and see if she wanted to go out, but after her friend's sorry state last weekend, she passed. Outside of Tori, Chelsea didn't have any other friends. At least not in Saddle Ridge. Except for Ryder. He counted as a friend.

She picked up her phone to text him. Her thumbs hovered over the keyboard. Ryder was probably still at dinner with Harlan, but that didn't mean she couldn't thank him one more time for today. Just a little message to show him she was thinking of him.

Chelsea turned the phone facedown on the table. No, he deserved uninterrupted time with his brother. She picked up her plastic TV dinner tray and carried it to the sink to rinse it off. Okay, that killed five seconds. Now what?

Her phone dinged from the table. She spun to face it as her pulse kicked into overdrive. Most likely her daughter had sent a text saying she was fine and having fun. Chelsea casually crossed the room, forcing every girlish emotion to remain in check. She flipped the phone over and saw one new message…from Ryder.

Can you talk?

Her hand trembled as she pressed the call button, bracing herself for a letdown.

"Hello?" Two syllables into the conversation and Chelsea already sensed his distress.

"I figured calling was easier than texting. How did your dinner go with Harlan?"

"Not well." He sighed. "I'm not interrupting you and Peyton, am I?"

"No. I'm alone. Peyton is spending the night with Missy. Do you want to come over?"

Why did she ask him that? She wasn't ready to be alone with him. At least not in her house. At night. With her bedroom only one floor away. Then again, who needed a bedroom? It had been so long she'd—she'd what? Take him on the couch? Here he needed someone to talk to, and she immediately thought about jumping his bones. Real classy, Chelsea.

"I'm not sure that's a good idea. I don't think your neighbors will approve."

"Approve of what? A black Jeep parked in my driveway. How many black Jeeps are there in Saddle Ridge, let alone the state of Montana? They won't think anything of it. If it'll make you feel better, I'll turn out the front light so no one will see you walk through my door."

Apparently her subconscious didn't have a problem with inviting him over even though she was doing everything she would advise a single parent client not to do:

Don't invite a man you barely know into your home.

Stay away from ex-convicts.

And more than anything else, trust your instincts. If it feels wrong, it is wrong.

Inviting Ryder over didn't feel wrong. Something had happened with his brother and he needed her. Not Tori, not some random stranger he could easily talk to in a bar…but her.

"If you're sure."

"I am." She gave him her address and hung up. She had a good fifteen minutes before he arrived. That gave her a chance to clean up a little. As she walked by the couch, her robe snagged on the end table. "Oh God, I need to change."

The first ache of today's outing reared its ugly head as she ran upstairs. Muscles she hadn't used in decades stiffened between her bath and now. In her bedroom, she unfastened her robe, allowing it to fall to the floor. She stood naked in front of her closet, three-quarters of which held work clothes. The rest seemed too casual. Too casual for what? She was home alone on a Sunday night. What did she think he expected her to answer the door wearing? An evening gown?

She tugged on a T-shirt and yoga pants, almost forgetting her bra. She didn't want to look that casual. After a quick swipe of mascara, she ran a brush through her hair just as the doorbell rang. What did he do... fly there?

Downstairs, she counted to three before opening the door. "Hi."

"Hi." Ryder stood on her doorstep in his usual faded jeans and cowboy boots. His tan barn jacket looked new and expensive, and she wondered how he afforded it fresh out of prison. His hat-free head surprised her most. She'd always seen him in a hat. But she'd never seen him this bare...and vulnerable. And he definitely looked vulnerable tonight. "May I come in?"

"Oh! I'm sorry." She stepped aside. "Are you all right? You sounded a little stressed over the phone."

Ryder stepped into her foyer and tugged off his boots, earning him instant brownie points. "I'll be fine. Dinner with my brother didn't go as expected."

"He didn't hit you, did he?"

Ryder laughed. "Nah, although I wish he had. It would have been better than him dredging up the night my dad died."

Chelsea stood there, waiting for him to continue. She suddenly didn't know what to do with her hands. Yoga pants didn't have pockets and crossing her arms felt judgmental. When he said nothing further, she walked toward the living room, assuming he'd follow. "Can I get you anything to drink, I don't have any beer, but I have wine, water or coffee."

"Coffee, black would be great. Thank you." Ryder stood in front of the fireplace mantel, looking at the framed photos of her family. "Is the little girl in this one you?"

"Which one?" Chelsea leaned across the kitchen peninsula to get a better view. Ryder held up the photo of her blowing out the candles on her fifth birthday. "That's me."

"You were a cute kid. Not that you're not cute now. Because you are. But you're more beautiful than cute."

Chelsea laughed to herself as she dropped a coffee pod into the machine. At least she wasn't the only nervous one. She grabbed a bottle of water from the fridge while his coffee brewed. "Make yourself at home out there. I'll just be a minute." She twisted off the cap and took a long swallow. *You can do this, Chelsea.* Talking to him alone in her house was no different from their car ride earlier. Only this time she wouldn't stick her foot in her mouth.

The coffeemaker released a final burst of steam as

if mocking her nervousness. "Here you go," she said as she padded out of the kitchen. "Do you want to talk about what happened with Harlan?" She tucked a leg beneath her as she sat next to him on the couch. "Or if you'd rather not, we can just watch TV."

Ryder sipped his coffee, wincing at the heat. He was buying time. Taking a moment to formulate the answer he thought she'd want to hear. She saw the tactic in the courtroom all the time. She reached for the remote, deciding for him. She refused to force him to talk if he wasn't ready. She'd learned that lesson earlier.

Ryder's hand covered hers. "Like you, Harlan believes there's more to what happened the night my father died."

"Is there?"

Ryder's eyes closed. "I hate remembering that night. There was so much going on between me and Tori, my mom and my dad, my dad and Wes."

"Wes? He was there that night?"

"No, he was on the road. Another rodeo somewhere. I never could keep up with his schedule. He was home as little as possible."

"Didn't he get along with your dad?"

"Dad had always been hard on him. Really hard. Despite Wes's success on the bull riding circuit, he never lived up to the man my father wanted him to be. You only need to spend five minutes with Wes to realize he doesn't play by anybody else's rules."

Chelsea let go of the remote and turned her palm upward, entwining her fingers with his. "You can't force a person to be someone they're not."

"That's just it. Back then, Wes was exactly like Dad. Hard, angry, determined, philandering."

"Your dad cheated on your mom?" Based on the way everyone in town treated Ryder, she'd assumed the Slades were the pinnacle of virtue. Between what Tori had told her and now this, she couldn't understand why anyone sang their praises.

"He had a romance going on with his ex-high school girlfriend. They'd both married other people, but they'd never quite gotten over each other. I used to pray my folks would get divorced. Dad would say he was going fishing with his buddies for the weekend and Mom would always find them together at some hotel miles from here."

"What did your brothers say about that?"

"I don't think Dylan and Garrett knew. They'd both married and moved out before things got really bad. No one knew. Maybe Wes did, maybe not. He kept his distance. My dad's affair was one of Saddle Ridge's best-kept secrets. I told Harlan though. He tried talking to Dad, but you couldn't reason with my father. He was right, you were wrong. No matter what the situation. Harlan and I both told Mom to leave but she wouldn't. She believed a half a loaf of bread was better than none. Those were her exact words."

"That had to have been awful to live with."

"You can't even imagine. Their marriage had significantly worsened by the time Tori and I got together—unbeknownst to us. When I moved back home, I saw just how bad it had gotten. That's what Tori and I walked in on the night he died. They were fighting once again, only Mom had reached her limit. She wanted out, but Dad wouldn't let her go. Tori and I both tried to stop the fight. Mom had been drinking, and Tori wanted to take her home to sober up. I just wanted to escape the madness."

"Is that when the accident happened?" Chelsea could see how his distress of that night would make him get behind the wheel, even though he'd been drinking.

Ryder opened his mouth as if he wanted to say more, but he didn't. He fell silent without acknowledging her question. That increasing uneasiness swelled within her. Now she was more positive than ever there was something he and Tori were hiding.

"Ryder, you can trust me. You can tell me anything."

"There's nothing more to say. It was an accident. I tried to stop it, but I couldn't. It happened so fast and then he was gone." He continued to stare across the room at the blank television screen as if he were watching a replay of that night.

He tried to stop it? Ryder's confession from the night of his father's death churned in her brain. Nowhere had it mentioned him trying to stop the truck. That gut instinct that propelled everyone's fight-or-flight response kicked in and the truth about that night hit her like a freight train. She knew in her heart something didn't sound right. Now she knew with every fiber of her being. Ryder hadn't killed his father, but he'd tried to stop the person who had.

Chapter 8

Ryder shot upright in bed. The clock on the bedside table read half past midnight. He rubbed his eyes, trying to force them to adjust faster to the darkness. Where was he? He patted the wall above him until he found the small light mounted above the bed and clicked it on. He was home. At least what had become his home. Had he dreamed going to Chelsea's?

Shadows loomed large in every corner of the small room. The three other beds sat empty, taunting him. He was alone. After spending five and a half years sharing a prison cell, he thanked every day he had the entire two-room bunkhouse to himself. Except for tonight. He hadn't wanted to be alone tonight.

But he hadn't been alone. He remembered sitting in Chelsea's living room and talking. About what? He swung his legs over the side of the bed, resting his elbows on his thighs. "What did I tell her?" He held his head in his hands, searching through the fog in his brain for answers.

The image of his mother behind the wheel of his father's truck and Ryder begging her to let him in flashed in his head. He could still feel the cold steel beneath his palms along with the sting from the thousand cuts he'd gotten from shattering the driver's side window.

He stood up and bolted for the bathroom. Blindly reaching past the thin shower curtain, he turned on the water and climbed in, not bothering to take off his clothes. He didn't want to remember that night. He didn't want to relive it again and again as he did every time he closed his eyes. His father's lifeless body lying on the ground behind the truck. His mother slumped over the steering wheel passed out cold. Tori screaming and him helplessly watching the last fragments of his family falling apart.

He wanted to save them both. But he couldn't. His father was already gone. He'd pulled his mother from the truck, frantically brushing the glass from her clothing and hair. He'd ordered Tori to get her inside, strip her down and get her in her nightgown and into bed. They bagged her clothes and tossed them in the trunk of Tori's car, fearing they held fragments of shattered glass. Ryder climbed behind the wheel of the truck and touched everything. He wanted his handprints everywhere. And then he crawled out…

He crawled beside his father and cried. The man had been a bastard on his worst days, but a loving man on his best. They hadn't seen eye to eye since Ryder's early teens and he despised him for the way he'd treated his mother; nevertheless, the man was his father. And he'd watched his mother kill him.

When the police arrived, he told them he'd done it despite Tori pleading with him not to. His mother already had a DUI on her record although Ryder doubted anyone other than he and his father knew about it. She'd gotten it a few years earlier in another county after catching his father with his mistress. Ryder had bailed her out of jail and even ran all her errands when she lost her license for six months. He'd blamed his father for driving her to drink when he should have been blaming himself for enabling her. Those six months would've been the perfect time to get her into rehab. To call out her addiction. To at least get her to an AA meeting. Instead, he ran to the liquor store for her, bringing her back anything she asked for. He was just as responsible for his father's death as she was.

Ryder shut off the water and sagged against the wall. The memories of that night had worsened since his release. At least when he'd been in prison, he'd been away from it. Nothing there had reminded him of home. Now he couldn't escape.

He grabbed the towel hanging from the hook next to the shower and wrapped it around his shoulders. His head ached as if he'd drunk too much. But he'd only had one beer with Harlan. Did he drink at Chelsea's? He remembered coffee but not driving home. He peeled off his wet jeans and left them on the shower floor. Wrapping the towel around his waist, he plodded through the kitchen and opened the front door. The Jeep was outside. Why couldn't he remember?

He retrieved his phone from the nightstand and scanned through the call log and text messages. He had texted Chelsea earlier and then she'd asked him over. He remembered that much. He remembered sitting next to her on the couch and watching television. A movie…they'd watched a movie. *Forrest Gump.* But there was something he was forgetting. He closed the front door and finished drying off. Once he dressed and made a cup of coffee, he sat down at the kitchen table and attempted to replay the night's events.

Dinner with Harlan had started great until his brother said he knew Ryder hadn't killed their father. Harlan had hedged about it when he'd visited him in prison, but he'd never outright asked like he had tonight. Ryder had covered for their mother all these years never once thinking anyone would've suspected Tori. But Harlan did. Ryder had brushed off the question and talked about the at-risk youth program instead, all the while worrying if his brother would pursue his suspicion further.

But he hadn't told Chelsea that, even though she already suspected he was hiding something. Did she think Tori was driving, too? Their conversation became clearer with each sip of coffee. He'd told her more about the night of the accident but kept it purposely vague even though he wanted nothing more than to unburden himself and tell her the truth. All of it. He remembered her hugging him and clinging to her for what seemed like an eternity. And then they'd watched the movie. He pictured saying goodbye at the door and even driving away from her house, but not coming home.

"Oh my God." He flattened his hands on the table. "I drove to Mom and Dad's ranch." Only the ranch hadn't belonged to his family in years. Ryder didn't even know who the new owners were. But that hadn't stopped him last night.

He closed his eyes, remembering...

Ryder turned off the Jeep's headlights as he drove onto the ranch, not wanting to wake anyone. Halfway to the house, he slammed on the brakes. A new addition sat on the very spot his father took his last breaths. They'd buried it, just as they'd buried his father. He stared through the windshield.

He could still see his parents fighting. Mom could barely stand, let alone heave the suitcase she dragged behind her into the bed of the truck. She was drunk again and didn't need to get behind the wheel. Dad was the last person she wanted to stop her. Not when she needed to get away from him most.

Ryder opened the door and climbed out. He had to get his mom back inside and in bed. Once she sobered up tomorrow, he'd drive her out to Dylan's in Billings and get her away from his dad for good. But he wasn't fast enough. She was behind the wheel of the truck, starting the engine.

"Mom, no!" he shouted. "Mom, stop!"

Dad ran behind the truck, as she revved the engine. "Bernadine, get out of there now."

"Stay away from her!" Ryder yelled. "Why couldn't you have left years ago?"

His father spun to face him and tripped, falling to the ground. The truck's white backup lights suddenly illuminated the parking area and then he heard that horrible bone-crunching sound.

"Dad! No!" Ryder fell to his knees, trying to crawl toward his father, but he wasn't there. He pressed his hands against the new addition, searching for what once was. Floodlights illuminated the front of the house and a tall slender man swung the screen door open so hard it smacked against the clapboard siding. He waved his fist in the air, shouting, "You kids get out of here! I'm tired of this shit!"

Ryder scrambled to his knees and ran toward the Jeep, grinding the gears as he threw it in Reverse and backed down the ranch drive. He pulled onto the main road and looked back at the parking area one last time. It had been his fault. If he hadn't yelled at his father, he never would have turned around and fallen.

"Why the hell is this happening now?" Ryder jumped up from the table, spilling his coffee. "Shit!"

The prison psychologist had diagnosed him with post-traumatic stress disorder shortly after his incarceration. It had taken years for him to accept he hadn't caused his father's death. And he'd gotten a handle on the nightmares and random memory flashes back then, too, but now they were out of control. "I never should've come back here." The draw to his family's ranch had been too great. He'd ignored it for days until finally, it overpowered him.

What harm would a visit do? That had been his logic. Go there, see it and move on. Only he wasn't moving on.

Hot coffee dripped off the table onto his bare feet, but he was numb to the pain. He grabbed a towel from the counter and mopped up the mess, cursing himself. He loved his mom, but some days he wished he hadn't made the sacrifice. The courts would have been harder on her. With only Ryder and possibly Wes backing up the years of abuse, he doubted she'd have received a fair trial. Him pleading guilty gave her the chance to clean up her life. Five and a half years in prison had been worth it. Hadn't they?

Ryder threw on his boots and jacket and stormed out of the bunkhouse. So what if it was only one thirty in the morning. He had work to catch up on since he'd spent so much time at the Bloodworth Ranch last week. He'd start with working on the tractor that desperately needed a tune-up. It needed to purr like a kitten once the snow fell. And in northwestern Montana that could be next week.

When noon rolled around, every muscle in his body ached. Good. Hard work meant he'd accomplished something. His stomach grumbled. He still needed to replace some tin sheathing on the main barn, but it would have to wait until after he grabbed something to eat. Maybe Chelsea was available for lunch. He felt the need to apologize to her for last night, although by the time he cleaned up and got into town it might be too late. Heck, it never hurt to try.

He saw Harlan's police SUV turn into the ranch parking lot as he tugged his phone out of his pocket. Two text messages from Chelsea and one missed call from Harlan. Wonderful. He'd forgotten to turn the ringer back on his phone.

His brother parked behind the Jeep, blocking him from leaving.

"Hey, you avoiding me?" Harlan said through the open window.

"I just saw you called. Sorry. What's up?" After last night, Ryder hoped this wasn't another inquisition.

"A complaint came in last night from the owner of our old ranch. The man said he chased someone driving a dark-colored Jeep off the property. Do I even have to ask if that was you?"

Ryder folded his arms and laughed. "What are you going to do, arrest me?"

Harlan squinted up at him from the driver's seat. "The fact you're driving a dark-colored Jeep is circumstantial, so no. Besides, half the kids in town drive Jeeps. I just want to know what's going on with you."

"I was only there for a few minutes."

Harlan opened the SUV's door, grabbed his hat from the passenger seat and stepped out of the vehicle. "Why did you go there? You were trespassing on private property."

"I had to." Ryder's skin prickled, and for a second he wondered if Harlan would arrest him. "I thought I could get it out of my system if I saw it one more time."

"I hope it's out of your system because if you get caught doing it again, you'll go directly to jail on a parole violation. Is that what you want?"

"I don't know." Ryder began to pace. He wanted to jump on a horse and ride for the rest of the day. No conversations. No interruptions. Just solitude with the best friend a man could ever have. "It was easier, man. In there I only had to deal with distant memories. Here it's in my face every day. You don't get it. You weren't there that night."

"If I had been, things would've been a hell of a lot different."

"Please don't start your conspiracy theories again." Ryder walked to the Jeep. "I can't deal with them today. Now, if you don't mind, I have someplace else I need to be."

"I came here for two reasons and I'm not sure if the second one will help you or hurt you."

Ryder slammed the Jeep's door. "What now?"

"A letter came in the mail for you this morning. It came to my house because she didn't know where else to send it."

"She?"

Harlan removed the letter from his inside jacket pocket and handed it to Ryder. "It's from Mom. I haven't opened it, but I can if you want me to."

Ryder stared at his mother's familiar handwriting on the plain white envelope. Neat and the picture of perfection. Exactly the way she and his father had portrayed their family to everyone.

"Or, we could just leave this for another day."

Harlan started to tuck the envelope back in his pocket when Ryder stopped him.

"No, I'll take it." He held out his hand. "I don't know why she wrote me now when I haven't heard from her in over five years."

"Make that three things I wanted to talk to you about."

Ryder sagged against the side of the police cruiser. How much worse could the day get?

"I had planned to talk to you about it last night, but since I pissed you off with my question, I decided to leave it for another day."

Ryder gestured for him to speed it up. "Tell me already, and while you're at it, tell me everything else you thought you should save for another day." His brother meant well, but Ryder was a "rip the Band-Aid off" type of guy.

"Mom's coming for a visit."

Ryder reached behind him to keep his knees from buckling. "Why now?"

"She wants to be here for Wes's wedding next weekend."

"But she didn't come to your wedding. Or Dylan's or Garrett's. You told me she didn't even come to her grandchildren's christenings. What is so special about Wes's wedding?"

"It's not about Wes. It's about you. She's coming back to Saddle Ridge because you're home. Her sons are finally all in one place again and she wants to see us all. Together."

"Thank you for inviting me over for dinner." Chelsea shrugged out of her coat and hung it on the hall tree next to Tori's front door. "My lunch consisted of a granola bar and I'm famished." She loved Tori and Nate's impromptu cookouts, especially after a long day in court. "I brought you a bottle of wine."

"We need to make this a weekly thing instead of always so last-minute. It's so hard to plan anything around Nate's schedule. I hope you don't mind, but we invited another couple to join us," Tori said as they walked toward the kitchen.

Another couple? Did that mean they'd invited Ryder, too? Not that she and Ryder were a couple. She'd only spoken with him for a few minutes this afternoon and his tone sounded strained. It had been the middle of the afternoon and she'd probably interrupted his job. She should've waited until the end of the day, but after last night, she wanted to check in on him.

The feeling he wanted to tell her more about the night his father died gnawed at her. Whatever happened, he definitely hadn't told her the complete truth. If he would only trust her, she could help him clear his name, because no matter how many times he said he was the driver that killed his father, she knew in her heart he wasn't. And Tori knew the truth.

When Tori invited her to dinner, Chelsea thought it would be the perfect opportunity to talk to her about it. Now not so much, since she'd invited another couple. It didn't matter. She'd wait however long it took, but one way or the other, she'd find out who really killed Frank Slade.

"Why would I mind? It's your home. I should've brought another bottle of wine."

"We have that covered." A tall slender woman with

warm golden-brown skin rose from her stool at the kitchen island holding a wine bottle of her own.

"Chelsea, this is Dr. Lydia Presley and her husband, Calvin. Lydia and Calvin, this is Chelsea Logan."

"It's a pleasure to meet you." Calvin offered his hand. "Your daughter is teaching our two boys sign language in the great room."

"It's wonderful to meet you, too." She shook both of their hands. "How old are your children?"

"Joshua is seven and Eli is nine." Lydia opened her bottle of wine with the corkscrew Tori handed her. "Would you like a glass?"

"Yes, please. I'm going to pop in the other room and say hello to my daughter real quick." Chelsea heard Peyton's laughter all the way in the kitchen. "I'll be right back."

She found Peyton sitting on the fireplace hearth holding class for her two eager students. The three of them were cute together. Joshua formed near-perfect signs while his older brother struggled a bit. She didn't want to interrupt them. It was the first time she'd seen her daughter teach another child how to sign. Her ability to speak made teaching that much easier, and if she hadn't had her heart set on becoming a veterinarian she'd make a great sign language teacher. Peyton had endless amounts of patience...except, at times, when it came to her mother.

She turned to leave when she saw Missy balled up on the couch, pouting. Chelsea sat beside the child and tapped her legs so she would look at her. "What's wrong? Don't you want to play with them?"

She shook her head violently. "No." She signed with force.

"Did they exclude you or did you decide not to join them on your own?"

"I don't want to play with them." Missy's expression darkened as her fingers sharply punctuated each word.

"Why not?"

"They asked me why I couldn't talk like Peyton."

By asking, Chelsea assumed one of the boys had written out their question on paper or on a cell phone. "Did you explain to them that not everyone in the deaf community can talk?"

"Peyton told them," Missy emphasized the word *told* and that confirmed what Chelsea had suspected. Missy associated strongly with the deaf community, refusing to take speech classes. She likely felt she shouldn't have to change the way she communicated to suit others. Peyton, having once been a hearing child, identified with both the deaf and hearing communities, and wanted to continue her education and work with hearing people. And for her that meant continuing to speak to them as she used to.

"Are you mad at Peyton, or are you mad at the situation?" Chelsea asked.

Missy shrugged and crossed her arms, ending further conversation.

"Okay, sweetie." Chelsea kissed the top of her head.

"Mommy?" Peyton tugged on her shirt. "I didn't mean to hurt Missy's feelings," she said as she signed.

"I know you didn't, but you have to let her answer for

herself when someone asks her a question. Just because you can speak, doesn't mean you should."

"But it was easier," Peyton argued.

"Easier isn't always better. You need to accept her way of communicating, the same way she's accepted yours." Missy had shown some outward animosity toward Peyton when they first met. Once Tori began watching her daughter after school, Missy realized Peyton needed to be taught many signs she hadn't learned yet. A year older, Missy began tutoring Peyton. Now Peyton was trying to pass that knowledge on to Joshua and Eli. "You need to let Missy teach them how to sign, too."

"Okay, I will."

Chelsea stilled her daughter's hands. "Without speaking for her. If she asks you for help, then that's fine. Otherwise, you let Missy teach them her way. Do you understand what I'm saying and why I'm saying it?"

Peyton nodded. Chelsea gave her a hug and left the four of them to work out their differences. Children usually found a way to overcome obstacles, sometimes much better than the adults that walked through her office door.

She turned the corner and smacked square into Ryder's chest. "Oh my God, Chelsea! I'm so sorry." He reached out to steady her. "Are you okay?"

"Talk about almost knocking a woman off her feet."

"I didn't hurt you, did I?"

The concern etched in Ryder's features made her smile and she fought the urge to reach up and stroke his cheek. It looked silky smooth, and she'd bet he'd just shaved for dinner. "I'm fine. I'm glad to see you."

"I'm glad to see you, too." He scanned the length of her body. "Especially when you're not wearing those narrow little suits of yours."

Chelsea straightened the sweater she had changed into after work. Ever since Ryder had told her she needed to cut loose, she made a point to run home and throw on something more comfortable before picking up Peyton from Tori's. That gave them a chance to go out afterward and do kid-friendly activities without Chelsea constantly saying she wasn't dressed for it.

"Hey, I have to wear those narrow little suits in court. I'm not a fan, but I'm definitely glad to get out of them at the end of the day. I heard what you said about cutting loose. I even took Peyton to one of those trampoline parks last week."

"I would've paid to see that." He waggled his brows.

"I bet." Chelsea smacked him playfully. His mood had definitely improved from last night. "Those places need to come with a big-busted-bounce warning."

"Yes, but I'm sure you bounced beautifully." Ryder lowered his voice. "Listen, I want to apologize for barging in on you last night."

"You didn't barge in, I invited you." Chelsea reached for his hands and held them between hers. "I'm available whenever you want to talk."

"Thank you, but there's nothing more to talk about as far as the night my dad died is concerned. I'm just trying to adjust to living back here and last night it got to me."

"And you're better now?" Chelsea doubted he'd worked out everything in a day.

"I'm getting there." He eased out of her grasp and she instantly missed his touch. "I'm not so sure I should be here. I'm worried about Peyton telling her friends, or Lydia and Calvin's kids saying something in school."

"What are they going to say? It's a group setting. There are six adults. The kids won't fixate on any one of us and I'm sure Eli and Joshua have no idea about your past. But just for the record…if Calvin and Lydia will sit down and have dinner with you, you were wrong about not having friends in Saddle Ridge."

Chelsea didn't wait for an answer. She grabbed his hand and led him back to the kitchen where Tori was telling Lydia and Calvin about the new not-so-nice words Missy had learned in school. "We all dread that day when our kids come home having learned one or two swear words from a friend, but Missy somehow learned all of them at once."

"Oh no!" Lydia gasped. "We haven't run into that yet, but I'm waiting for it."

"Do you mind me asking if Peyton was born deaf?" Calvin asked. "She speaks perfectly."

"She lost her hearing three years ago after contracting osteomyelitis due to an infection caused by the surgery she had for a broken leg." The sentence had become second nature to her after having to repeat it to almost everyone they met.

"That had to have been incredibly difficult for both of you." Lydia's sympathetic tone was a welcome change from the pitying ones she'd received from many parents of hearing children.

"It almost killed me to watch her go through it all. So many changes in her life. She went from the top of her class to the bottom in a matter of months. There's no correcting her hearing. She will always be deaf." Chelsea sipped the wine Lydia handed her, swallowing down the words that pained her every time she spoke them. "I enrolled her in the deaf school near where we lived in Helena, but she couldn't grasp the lessons because she didn't understand the language. She had to learn to communicate first to continue her education. The school almost left her back a year, but they set us up with a wonderful tutor that worked with her every single day after school. She still has a long road ahead of her. Missy is much more advanced in her sign language skills than Peyton."

"It's hard watching your kid struggle." Tori set a plate of hot nachos on the center of the island. "Dig in everyone," she said, taking a seat again. "Missy doesn't want to learn how to speak or read lips. As a parent that really frustrates me. I want to see her succeed in talking to both deaf and hearing people, and grow as a person, but the decision about how she chooses to communicate is hers and hers alone. I can't tell you how many times she's told me I don't understand. And she's right."

"Let me tell you, reading lips comes with its own set of problems." Chelsea laughed. "Peyton has slowly been learning how to do it and practicing by eavesdropping on conversations across the room. We've had more than one discussion about that. Especially when they're my conversations she's eavesdropping on." She lifted a gooey nacho onto her napkin, allowing it to cool. "But reading lips will come in handy if she travels internationally, which she wants to do. She'll be able to read lips to a certain extent in English-speaking countries, but she'll be hindered by foreign pronunciations and accents. That being said, almost every country has its own version of sign language. It's quite different from spoken languages. When you learn Spanish, it's Spanish regardless of where you go in the world, aside from the regional dialects. But sign language is much more complex. It's limiting for an adult, and I imagine it's intimidating for a child."

"So, if Peyton traveled abroad, she couldn't use sign language unless she learned that country's version of it?" Calvin asked.

Chelsea nodded as she chewed her nacho. "They only use American Sign Language in the United States and most of Canada. Australia uses Auslan Signbank. England and Scotland, where Peyton wants to study equine medicine, uses British Sign Language, which is completely different. Not only that, if she goes to Ireland, they have their own sign language, as well."

"Peyton wants to be an equine veterinarian?" Lydia asked. "I'm a large animal vet. I'd be happy to talk to her about it."

Chelsea smiled at her. "That would be wonderful. I'm sure my daughter would love that."

"I've met a few deaf veterinarians over the years. There's one equine vet out of North Carolina who I consult with on a regular basis. I can give you her name and contact information, if Peyton would be interested in talking to her, too."

"That'd be great. Thank you." Chelsea had wanted to reach out to one of the veterinarians in town but hadn't gotten around to it yet. It was one more thing that had fallen by the wayside because she brought her work home with her. That had to stop.

"No problem." Lydia reached for her bag and pulled out a business card. "Here's my info. How much experience does Peyton have with horses?"

She honestly didn't know. Her daughter spent every weekday on the ranch and Chelsea hadn't taken the time to explore that world with her. Peyton talked about the horses and donkeys every day, but as to actual hands-on experience with them, she didn't have an answer. Another thing that had to change.

Tori met her eyes across the island. "I've taught her some basic horse care…grooming, hoof cleaning, feeding schedules." Things Chelsea should have known and didn't. "And she's gone riding with Nate, Missy and me a few times. We haven't managed to get Chelsea up on a horse yet, though."

"You don't like to ride?" Ryder asked, sounding like a crestfallen kid who just found out Santa didn't exist.

Chelsea handed Lydia her card after taking the other woman's. "I didn't say that. I can't tell you if I do or if I don't. I haven't been on a horse since I was a kid and even then, it was on a pony at a campground where someone led me through a trail."

"Ryder, you need to take her riding this weekend," Tori said matter-of-factly, as if Chelsea had no say whatsoever. "We have some nice trails behind the sanctuary."

"Thanks for the help, Tori." Ryder rolled his eyes. "If you had given me a chance, I would have asked her myself. Like maybe someplace a little more private." He turned to Chelsea and smiled, exposing those swoon-worthy dimples she couldn't get enough of. "Chelsea, would you like to go riding with me this weekend?"

There was nothing like putting her on the spot in front of everyone. "Sure, I would love to."

Nate entered the kitchen with a large stainless-steel tray of grilled steaks, salmon and vegetables. He set it on the counter for Tori and she began arranging the platters.

"Congratulations, you two." Calvin raised his wine glass. "You have officially fallen under Tori's match-making prowess. Before long, you'll be married with two kids. Trust me, I speak from experience."

"Tori got you and Lydia together?" Chelsea asked, desperate to shift the focus from her and Ryder. As of yesterday, they were *exploring*—whatever that was supposed to mean—and now she wondered if horseback riding was a continuation of that exploration or an actual date.

Nate grabbed two beers from the fridge and handed one to Ryder.

"I never knew that." Ryder twisted off his bottle cap.

"It was Tori's and my senior year in high school. I was a cheerleader and Calvin played football for a rival team. Tori saw us flirting across the field and not only got his number, she set up the entire date and surprised us both with it. But it's not like we got married right away. It took Calvin seven years to propose."

"That's because you always had your nose buried in a book." Calvin wrapped an arm around his wife and gave her a sweet kiss on the cheek. "Speaking of books and school… Does the public school here offer sign language? I wonder if Josh and Eli would be interested in taking a class after their lesson tonight." He smiled.

"No, the school doesn't but it should," Nate said as he took one of the platters and walked toward the dining room. "Especially since we have a deaf school in the same town. Who's hungry?"

Ryder rounded up the children from the great room and ushered them to the table. Chelsea sat across from him, loving how he picked up on the girls' tension and plunked himself down between them, conversing not only with Missy and Peyton but with Eli and Joshua too. He managed to make all four children equally comfortable while still talking to the adults at the table. He even made Missy smile.

Nate always seemed to have one eye on him, and Chelsea still couldn't understand why he had agreed to let Ryder move onto the ranch if he wasn't comfortable with him being around. On the outside, he was friendly to Ryder, then there were the side glances and an undercurrent of jealousy that made her uneasy. Tori may need Ryder to stay on the ranch, but she hoped Drew or anyone else offered him a permanent place elsewhere. The distance would do the James family some good.

When the Presleys left a few hours later, Chelsea began gathering Peyton's things from last night's sleepover so they could head home too. She hated leaving...leaving Ryder...but it was getting late and Peyton had school in the morning.

Ryder came into the great room and began helping her straighten up. The casualness in which he automatically fell into step with having children around both warmed and broke her heart. It couldn't be easy watching the child he raised live with another man. She saw Missy use name signs for Nate and Ryder and wondered if she had ever referred to Ryder as Daddy. But she didn't dare ask. It was none of her business and Ryder had enough memories to deal with without her adding one more.

"I had fun tonight. I'm glad Tori set it up."

"So am I." Ryder took Peyton's knapsack from Chelsea and set it on the couch. "I just wish we could all meet in town for dinner sometime or go to Oktoberfest without repercussions."

"It won't always be like this." Chelsea felt sorry for Ryder, although she wouldn't dare utter the words. Here he was a free man and he still couldn't walk down the streets of his own hometown. "In time people's perceptions will change."

"What if they never do? Don't get me wrong, I like the Bloodworth Ranch so far. It's an incredible program for both the parolees and the kids, but I can't see it changing anyone's mind about me."

"Then maybe you shouldn't live in Saddle Ridge. I get that your family is here, and you want to make things right with them. And your obligation to Tori is admirable, but you're not only doing yourself a disservice, you're doing Tori and Nate a disservice, too. Despite what she's said about their marriage, I get the feeling he's not thrilled you're here."

"I realize this isn't a permanent solution. My eyes are wide open for other jobs and I even asked Harlan to put feelers out for me. If another one comes up, I'll leave here. And you're right…it may not be in Saddle Ridge, but—"

"Are you talking about quitting?" Tori walked into the room with Nate close behind. "Ryder, you can't do that."

"Tori, you can't force the man to stay here," Nate said. "We'll figure out how to afford someone else. Even if we have to hire two part-timers."

Tori's eyes darted between her and Ryder. "Whose idea was it for you to quit?"

"I just think—"

Ryder stepped slightly in front of Chelsea, cutting her off. "Mine. And I'm not saying I'm quitting tomorrow, but staying here…living and working this close to my parents' old ranch is too much. When I accepted this job, I didn't realize it was on the same road as theirs. When I go in and out of town, I drive way in the opposite direction to avoid passing the place. Last night I couldn't avoid it anymore."

Tori slowly sat down on the couch. "Ryder, you didn't."

"I did. And I got caught. The new owner had no clue it was me, but Harlan figured it out when he looked over the incoming calls from last night. Judging by the way the guy yelled at me, I'm not the only one who has trespassed on his property to get a look at the infamous Slade death site."

"Honestly, I don't know how you do it." Nate sat next to his wife. "I wouldn't be able to live anywhere near the place. And I'm not just saying that because I want you to go."

"You want him to go?" Tori twisted and glared at him.

"Yeah, I do. But not for the reason you think." Nate leaned forward resting his arms on his knees. "I think Ryder and I both knew his living here would be awkward. That aside, I want him to go because—believe it or not—I actually do like you. I don't see how you can have a normal productive life with your father's death hanging over you. Get away from it…get away from here because the constant reminder of what happened is slowly killing you."

Chelsea wanted to believe Nate's sincerity, but there was something about the way he said the last sentence that made her wonder if he was hiding something, too. Whenever she was in the room with Nate lately, she felt like the three of them were in on a secret and she was the only one left out. She still didn't believe Ryder had been the driver the night his dad died. Could it have been Tori?

"When Harlan stopped by earlier today, he dropped off a letter for me from my mom."

"She wrote you?" Tori jumped off the couch. "What did she say?" Her eyes immediately shot to Chelsea. "Never mind, it's none of my business. I should go get the kids. They're up in Missy's room."

"I haven't read it yet. I wanted to do that tonight. Here with you."

Ryder's words froze Tori midstep. "Y-you do?" She asked as she slowly turned around.

"With all of you." Ryder corrected and pulled the folded envelope from his back pocket. "I just can't do it on my own. Will you read it out loud for me?" He handed it to Chelsea.

"Oh, Ryder." She took the envelope and ran her fingers over the worn creases. He must have folded and refolded it a hundred times. "Are you sure you want me to read something so personal…in front of everyone?"

"I—I don't think this is a good idea." Tori tried to reach for the letter, only to have Nate grab her hands and lead her back to the couch.

"This is Ryder's decision."

"I don't know what's in that letter, but I know I don't want to read it alone." He sat down on the other couch and patted the cushion next to him. "It's okay. I want you to do this. I'm ready."

Chelsea joined him and slid her finger under the envelope's flap, breaking the seal. "Okay, I'll read it for you." She unfolded three neat, handwritten pages and turned to Ryder. She wiped a tear from her cheek as she began. She'd read hundreds of letters like these for clients, but she'd never been personally involved with the intended recipient.

"My Dearest Ryder,

"Please forgive me for not writing sooner. The only excuse I can offer is the guilt I felt for living my life while you were locked away in that dreadful place. A

place you should never have been. You wouldn't have gotten behind the wheel of that truck if I hadn't created the pain you were so desperately trying to escape. I wish you had never pled guilty. I wish you hadn't waived your right to an attorney and had stood trial. I would have supported you. I would have told the court and the world what I had kept secret for so long...that your father and I were alcoholics and you'd walked in on another one of our fights."

"Dad was an alcoholic?" Ryder asked. "He couldn't have been. I would have known. I would have seen it."

Chelsea gave his hand a squeeze as she skimmed over the letter. "I think this next part will make things clearer."

"I'm sorry. Please continue." Ryder perched on the edge of the couch and stared down at the floor.

"*I know this is a shock for you to read. It will be for your brothers, too. I'm sending them separate letters two days after mailing yours. You deserved to learn the truth first since you've paid the biggest price.*

"*My alcoholism was no secret to you because I was sloppy and leaned on you for support. Your father despised that. He saw it as a sign of my weakness, but in truth, he feared it would expose him for the alcoholic he was as well.*

"*Frank hid his disease better only in the fact that no one else knew he had a problem. But every fight, every affair, every time he yelled at you kids was because he'd either had too much to drink or was battling withdrawal. The man he became was not the man I married or even the man he was during the first ten*

*or so years of your lives. He had been a loving father
and husband, willing to do anything for his family. Until
the day he caught me having an affair. Yes, son, I had
an affair first."*

"I can't believe this." Ryder stood and paced the
length of the room. "My mom had an affair. With who?"

"That's the next part." Chelsea looked up at him.
"Are you sure you don't want to read the rest of this by
yourself? It's extremely personal."

"No." He shook his head. "Please." He motioned to
the letter but remained standing in the middle of the
room.

Tori drew her knees to her chest as Nate wrapped an
arm around her, pulling her close.

*"The details of who or why no longer matter. What
matters is I was the trigger. I had already been drinking. Started when you boys were only toddlers. A nip
here, a nip there. Pretty soon those nips became bottles.*

*"Your father should have called me out. Oh Lord
how I wish he had, but I begged and pleaded with him
not to. And then I cheated. His stubborn pride refused
him to allow anyone else to know what I had done. I
broke our wedding vows, broke him and thus began
the destruction of our family. Where I drank to drink,
Frank drank to forget the pain I caused him, therefore
inflicting his own brand of personal hell. By the time
you moved back home after your marriage ended, our
marriage was in name only. Neither one of us had been
strong enough to walk away...until the night of your father's death.*

"My details of that night are sketchy at best. Things

*I thought I remembered turned out to be only a dream.
Alcohol addiction does that to you. But I do remember
your father and I sitting down that afternoon and deciding to end our marriage. We couldn't do it anymore.
Wes wouldn't come home. You were miserable, and we
knew Dylan, Garrett and Harlan would learn the truth
soon enough. We were slowly killing each other, and it
was only a matter of time before you or someone else
called the police on us. We had made the right decision.
We needed help, but we needed to get help separately."*

Ryder crouched on the floor and covered his face.
Chelsea's gaze met Nate's, and he nodded for her to
continue.

*"I saw your father cry for the first time that night. He
loved you boys so much and the guilt of how he treated
you ate away at his soul. He loved me, too, even after
what I'd done. So we opened one more bottle. Had one
more drink. And ended our marriage.*

*"If you know anything about alcoholics, you know it
doesn't end at one drink. Or one bottle. We drank. We
cried. And your father begged me to stay. But I couldn't.
That's where things begin to fade for me. I believe this
is when you came home. I remember you yelling and
Tori screaming. I remember Frank pulling me back in
the house, and then it goes black.*

*"You got in the truck that night to escape the pain we
had created. It wasn't your fault. It was ours. Ryder, I
need you to forgive yourself for that night, just as I for-
gave you. I can only ask for your forgiveness in return,
but I'll understand if that's not possible.*

"I've spent years working on my recovery. It's a

*never-ending process, but I can honestly say I've been
sober since that dreadful night. After receiving an invitation to Wes's wedding, I decided this was the right
time to see the five of you since you're all living in
Saddle Ridge again. It's my hope that these letters will
bring you boys together, so you can celebrate your ever-
growing families as a family. I'll be staying with Harlan beginning Friday, October 5. I'm coming alone,
and my stay is open-ended. I pray I'll see you there,
alongside your brothers.*

"I love you with all my heart. Just as your father did.

"Mom."

Chelsea refolded the pages and tucked them back
in the envelope. Ryder slowly rose to his feet, his eyes
glassy with tears he refused to cry.

"I don't believe this," Tori said from behind her
hands. "She doesn't remember."

"She remembers everything she needs to remember."
Ryder nudged the ottoman and sat down on it in front
of her. "She may not remember how we helped her that
night, but she remembered everything leading up to it.
Things I could never have imagined. It doesn't matter
now what she's forgotten."

And there it was. The knowing glance shared
amongst the three of them. But it was Ryder's words
that told her everything she needed to know: she may
not remember how we helped her that night… Bernadine Slade ran over her husband. Ryder was innocent.

Chapter 9

Tori's pickup truck spit and sputtered all the way to the auto parts store. And so did Ryder, only he was spitting and sputtering four-letter words. "How the hell did Tori even drive this thing?" He didn't know when it last had a tune-up, but today was its lucky day. It didn't matter if it took him all night. At least it would keep his mind off his brothers and the shock they were about to receive. As much as he wanted to warn them, to cushion the blow somehow, they needed to hear it from their mother. Not him.

It had been three days since Chelsea read his mother's letter. He'd wondered if it had held a confession exonerating him, but she'd only confirmed what he'd already known in his heart. She didn't remember driving the truck. The guilt would have killed her if she had. And he'd had five and a half years to make peace with the fact he'd done the right thing.

Harlan had asked what the letter said, but Ryder told him he wasn't ready to talk about it. He wanted his brothers to have the chance to read and absorb their own letters before discussing it. Just because his mother had said she'd mail them two days later didn't mean she had. Especially when you factored in the weekend. They'd arrive soon if they arrived at all. Maybe she'd chickened out or maybe she wanted to tell everyone in person when she arrived tomorrow.

Ryder still couldn't believe she was coming home. He'd tentatively accepted Harlan's invitation to dinner, figuring he'd gauge his brothers' reactions at the door. If it looked bad, he'd walk away.

A half hour later, Ryder had a crate full of parts, oil, fluids and filters. By the time he finished, Tori's demon on wheels would purr like a kitten. He almost finished crossing the parking lot when he saw Wes standing by the tailgate of the truck. Hesitating for a second, he wondered if his brother was moments away from punching him again.

"I come in peace." Wes held up his hands in surrender as Ryder dropped the crate in the bed of the truck.

"Were you looking for me or is this meeting just a coincidence?"

"I went to the ranch first and Tori told me you'd headed into town. I drove around until I found you."

"You can put your hands down, Wes." Ryder looked around the parking lot. "People will think I'm robbing you. I have a bad enough reputation around here as it is."

"I read Mom's letter."

Ryder pushed his hat back, trying to gauge his brother's reaction, but he'd always been good at remaining emotionless. It had come in handy around their father.

"Did she tell you she sent me one, too?"

Wes nodded. "I had no idea about Dad. Did you?"

"Not the faintest idea. He hid it well." Ryder still didn't know how he'd missed the signs of their father's alcoholism, especially since he could tell his mother had been drinking by looking at her. He'd seen the man with a drink on occasion, but he'd never appeared outwardly drunk. Of course there had always been liquor in the house, but he'd always assumed that was Mom's. He'd heard the phrases *closet alcoholic* and even *functioning alcoholic* before. Now he understood them. "Did she tell you about the affair?"

"Hers or his?" Wes asked.

"Both."

Wes nodded. "Out of all the fights they'd had, you'd think we would have heard she'd had an affair. Especially when she threw Dad's in his face all the time. I thought about this a lot last night. There were signs, but we missed them. I mean, look at Dad. You can pinpoint when he changed. That summer Uncle Jax stayed with us."

"Mom and Uncle Jax?" The man had been like a second father to all of them. He'd even visited Ryder in prison. "It couldn't have been."

"Think about it. Things were never right after that summer."

Ryder remembered camping and fishing trips that

summer…just with his brothers and their dad. "Oh my God. When Uncle Jax stayed behind with Mom."

"Exactly." Wes slapped the side of the pickup truck. "That had to have been what happened. It must have shattered him. His wife and his brother. The two people he should have been able to trust more than anyone."

"That doesn't make him blameless. He should have divorced Mom. Or if Mom had been that unhappy that she had felt the need to screw around, she should have divorced Dad. They're both at fault."

Ryder wanted to scream. He and Wes had taken the brunt of their parents' stubborn, foolish pride. Two people who had once loved each other so deeply had turned their lives into a living hell.

"Maybe they stayed because they thought they could make it work."

"We can't make assumptions about them." He'd spent most of his life doing just that. "The only way we'll get that answer is by asking Mom."

"How is that supposed to work? She flies into town tomorrow, and we say, 'Hey Mom, good to see you, why did you and Dad stay in a loveless marriage'?"

Ryder nodded. "Exactly. That's exactly what we do. I spent five and a half years in jail because our parents couldn't get it together. Mom wants forgiveness, I want answers."

"I can't put all the blame on them. I kept taking off because I couldn't deal with the fights anymore. Every single thing was a fight down to how much ketchup I put on my scrambled eggs in the morning." Wes threw his hands in the air. "I feel guilty for staying away and leaving you to deal with it and I feel guilty for feeling relieved once it was over." He swiped at his eyes. "I was a coward. I ran and hid."

"No, don't say that." Ryder would never blame his brother for wanting to escape the hell that had become their family. "You didn't hide. No one hides on the back of a bull. You were making a life for yourself. There was nothing wrong with that."

"I'm sorry for the way I've treated you."

"Wes, you don't have to apologize."

"Yes, I do, because I'm so angry at myself for believing you ran over Dad on purpose. I know you said it was an accident, but in the back of my mind you did it on purpose, maybe in a flash of anger, and I couldn't forgive you. But if I'm being honest with myself, deep down I was also glad. I was glad you did something when I couldn't. And none of it was your fault. None of it was Mom's fault and none of it was Dad's fault. It was because they had a damned disease and it took over their lives. Our lives."

"Wes, you have to stop. This ends with us. You and I were the last two to live in that house. We can either spend the rest of our lives beating ourselves up for missing the signs or accept we now know the truth. I'm assuming if you received your letter then Harlan, Dylan and Garrett received theirs. Now we all know what happened between Mom and Dad, and how it affected us. Once and for all, can we just put an end to the nightmare?"

Wes pulled him into a hug. "Yeah, it's over. It's over." He patted Ryder on the back and released him. "I'm getting married in a little over a week, and I'd really like you to be there. Harlan's my best man and Dylan and Garrett are my groomsmen, but I'd like you to be up there, too."

Ryder hadn't expected an invitation let alone to be a part of the ceremony. He'd fully intended on sneaking onto the Silver Bells Ranch and watching from afar, but this…it was more than he ever could have hoped for.

"I would be honored to be your groomsman."

"Oh, and this Sunday we're having a big family get-together at the ranch. A pre-wedding celebration, why don't you come and bring Chelsea. I don't know what the story is between you two, but Belle and Harlan say she's really nice. Besides, you need to meet my kids."

He didn't know what Chelsea was either. They hadn't spoken since the night she'd read the letter. He'd asked her for time to process everything and she'd told him to call her when he was ready. He finally felt hope for the future and he'd love her to be a part of it.

"I'll be there."

Ryder had thought all this would be over the day he walked out of the state penitentiary, but it hadn't truly ended until now. He had his brother back. And hopefully Dylan and Garrett would follow suit. They had never carried the animosity Wes had, but they'd kept their distance. Tomorrow they'd have their mom. And maybe they'd have all the answers they needed.

"Did I just see what I think I saw?" Chelsea called across the parking lot as Ryder slid behind the wheel of the pickup. She'd waited for Wes to leave before crossing the street.

"Where did you come from?" Ryder stood, bracing himself on the door.

"I was leaving the office supply store when I saw you." The strain from the past few days had left dark shadows beneath his eyes. "I won't ask you what Wes said but judging by what I saw, you two have made some progress."

"Better than that, he asked me to be a groomsman with my brothers at his wedding next weekend."

"That's wonderful!" Chelsea reached up and gave him a hug. "It's finally happening. You're getting everything you wanted. I'm so happy for you."

"Almost everything." He spun her around until her back was against the open door. Wordlessly he guided her to the edge of the driver's seat, shielding her from the rest of the world's view. "I've wanted to do this for a long time and now I feel like I finally can."

His mouth claimed hers as his soft, yet demanding lips echoed his words. His tongue urged her to open to him, melding them as one with each gentle stroke. Chelsea gripped his shirt, wanting to pull him closer. Wanting to show him how he made her feel. But the parking lot of an auto parts store wasn't the place and the middle of the afternoon wasn't the time.

"Ryder," she panted, needing to create some distance between them. "I have to get back to work." She silently prayed the short walk to the office would give her a chance to cool down.

"I'm sorry. I just couldn't wait another minute to do that." Ryder stepped away from the door frame, giving her the chance to adjust her skirt. "And for the record… I have more exploration in mind."

"So that's what we're still calling this?" She straightened and stepped away from the truck.

"Yeah, about that… Wes invited us to a big family get-together on Sunday at the Silver Bells Ranch. Wes, Garrett and Dylan own the place together. My entire family will be there including all my nieces and nephews, some of whom I've never met. I would love it if you and Peyton went with me. We can even go horseback riding."

"Yes! That sounds great. I look forward to meeting your family."

"Good, then it's a date." Ryder leaned forward and whispered in her ear, "From now on, I consider everything we do together a date."

"I think I can live with that." Chelsea's body thrummed thinking about all the other things they could do on their dates. "Listen, I promised Peyton I would take her to that pizza place arcade in Kalispell tonight. Would you like to meet us there? We could blow off some steam."

"I haven't been to that place since I was a teenager. I used to love it there." Ryder's dimples made her heart flutter every time she saw them. "Are you sure it's a wise idea for me to be around Peyton like that? What if she says something to her friends?"

"I think meeting you there will make it more of a casual outing. I'm not too worried about her saying anything to her friends anymore. Once people see you with your brothers at the wedding, the rest of the town will quickly come around. How could they not?"

"I hope you're right." He smoothed a piece of her hair back into place. "It will be nice to return to some semblance of normal."

"Besides, like I told you the other night, not everyone hates you. I think that may be more your perception and the guilt you've been carrying. Once you see your mother, a lot of that may go away."

"Speaking of my mother, I'm going to Harlan's tomorrow night to see my mom and my brothers. I would invite you—"

"Oh no." Chelsea shook her head. "I would never dream of intruding on that moment. If you need to talk afterward, I'm available. Peyton has an overnight school trip. The first one I'm not chaperoning, but Tori is so I'm okay with it. At least that's what I keep telling myself."

"I might take you up on that." Ryder kissed her lightly on the mouth, then spun her away from him. "Now go to work before we both get in trouble."

"I'll text you about tonight a little later," Chelsea called over her shoulder.

"Sounds like a plan."

If she hadn't been wearing three-inch heels, she probably would've skipped all the way back to the office. She ducked into the ladies' room before heading to her desk, wanting to make sure she didn't look like the wild, wanton woman raging inside her. No man had ever made her heart race and ache at the same time. Hopefully after this weekend he'd be more willing to open up and tell her the truth about the night his father died. Because now more than ever, she was determined to clear his name.

* * *

"Mommy, look! Ryder's here."

Peyton's enthusiasm erased any second thoughts she'd had about inviting him tonight. She didn't want her daughter to feel she had to compete for her attention, but she wanted to see the two of them interact without anyone else they knew around.

"What do we have here?" Ryder signed as he straddled the metal picnic-style bench and faced Peyton. "Just two of the most beautiful girls I've ever seen."

"What are you doing here?"

"I came to play the video games. Especially the motorcycle one over there." He pointed across the room to a life-size white-and-green racing bike. "You should see me on that thing."

"I've never been on that one." Peyton looked up at her. "Can I ride it?"

"I don't think you weigh enough to maneuver that one."

"But you do. We can ride it together."

"Yes, Chelsea." Ryder bounced on his bench. "You can ride it together."

"I don't know how to play that game, let alone ride a motorcycle." Chelsea had never been on one, real or fake.

"Guess what?" Ryder asked. "Today you're going to learn."

"Let's ride it now." Peyton jumped up from the table and ran across the arcade.

Ryder winked as he helped Chelsea up from the table. She loved his chivalry and his need to protect the ones he cared about. "Is this what I have to look forward to? You always taking her side."

"Hey, when the kid is right, the kid is right."

"Come on!" Peyton shouted to them.

"Oh! We better hurry." Ryder grabbed her hand and led her through the throng of pint-size humans. "Who wants to go first?"

"Mommy does." Peyton hopped from one foot to the other.

"Did Tori give you a lot of sugar this afternoon?" Chelsea hadn't seen her daughter this bubbly since before she lost her hearing.

"No. I'm just happy."

Chelsea didn't dare ask why. There was no reason to analyze it like she'd overanalyzed everything for the past however many years. She doubted it was any one thing that had put the smile on her child's face, but rather a combination of things that had begun falling into place. For the first time since they moved to Saddle Ridge, they'd found a balance in their lives. And whether or not Ryder played a part in that remained to be seen, but she liked where it was going.

"Hop on." Ryder patted the motorcycle seat.

"Shouldn't you go first and demonstrate how it's done?"

"Will that make you feel better?" Chelsea sensed a bit of mischief behind Ryder's challenging grin.

"Yes, it would." Chelsea fished two tokens out of her pocket and slid them into the machine. She patted the seat. "Hop on, hotshot."

For a man who spent five and a half years away from

all things motorcycle and video-game related, he beat the reigning high score on the first try.

"Next." He bent slightly at the waist and dramatically waved his arm to the side like an usher.

Chelsea swung her leg over the back of the bike, almost taking out her knee in the process. Coordinated she was not. Ryder dropped two tokens in the slot and the plastic bike began to shake. She immediately reached for the back of her shirt and tucked it into her jeans. "I can only imagine how attractive this must look from behind."

"Damn hot, if you ask me," Ryder winked. "Grab both handles." Ryder signed for Peyton as he spoke. "The right side is your throttle. Twist it toward you to increase your speed. Don't forget to use your hand brakes to slow down. When you see a turn, lean into it to maintain your speed, but don't lean too much or else you'll wipe out."

Lean? Wipe out? Throttle? For a video game, it all seemed too real. She watched the large screen in front of her as she twisted the rubberized handgrip. The motorcycle jerked and bounced beneath her as she drove over railroad tracks.

"Increase your speed, you're going to stall."

Chelsea came to a turn, forgot to lean and crashed into a parked car.

"Why didn't you slow down?" Ryder asked.

"Because you told me to increase my speed."

"On the straightaway. Not on a turn." He shook his head while Peyton laughed. "Do you want to give it another shot?"

Chelsea attempted to dismount the bike, almost falling on her butt. Maybe horseback riding this weekend wasn't such a good idea. If she couldn't handle something that was bolted to the floor, she didn't know how she'd handle riding something that moved.

"Mommy, you have to stay on for me to ride."

"Oh no I don't." Chelsea shook her head. "Ryder can teach you."

"Are you sure?" Surprise was evident in his eyes.

"She wants to have fun. Show her how to play the game the way it should be played. Only you can teach her that."

"Thank you for trusting me." He helped Peyton onto the motorcycle then climbed on behind her. He leaned forward and placed both hands on hers. They'd both have to trust each other to communicate without words. Without sign language.

Chelsea dropped two more tokens into the game and hit the start button. Her daughter's smile widened with each turn. Her laughter increased as the motorcycle accelerated. Ryder guided her through the imaginary course looking as if he enjoyed it as much as Peyton did. It was the first time Chelsea saw her with a father figure outside of Peyton's grandfather. She'd asked about her biological father numerous times and Chelsea couldn't give her any answers. How do you tell a child the person who helped create them wanted nothing to do with them? Most of her friends had fathers. They may not still be married to their mothers, but they knew who their fathers were. Even though she'd never said she was sad or upset about not having one, her sadness crushed

Chelsea whenever she saw Peyton watching other kids with their fathers. Chelsea would love to one day give her that gift. And once she convinced Ryder to clear his name, they'd have that chance.

Chapter 10

Ryder heard his mother's voice inside Harlan's house before his foot hit the first porch step. He hesitated, then started again when he heard someone come up behind him.

"Hey, little brother." Dylan, the oldest of his siblings, stood behind him, hands buried deep in his pockets. "I don't know what to say except I'm sorry."

"Don't." Ryder held up his hand. "I don't want us to sit around apologizing all night. Especially not to me. What's done is done. I don't hold any grudges or have any animosity toward anyone anymore. It's over."

"Do you really mean that?" his mother said through the open screen door. "Because I would love nothing more than to hear you say you forgive me."

The face of the woman who raised him had grown thinner and gaunter in the years he'd been away. Her shoulders appeared narrower, her hair grayer. Lines of time had etched into the skin around her eyes and lips. And yet, she was still the mother he remembered and loved.

"I forgive you, Mom." Ryder bounded up the stairs and embraced the woman he'd given up his freedom for. Holding her in his arms made everything he'd done worth it. "It's over."

"Maybe it is for you, but I have a lot of questions." Garrett walked up the stone path leading to the porch. "For starters, I want to know how come all this was going on and Harlan and I didn't know about it. Dylan I can understand. He wasn't living here then. But Harlan and I lived in the same damn town. Why didn't you or Wes come to me? Come to us? And Mom...you had five sons you could have turned to and you didn't."

Dylan placed a hand on Garrett's chest. "This isn't the time."

"Bullshit! That right there...that line of thinking is why two of my brothers suffered at the hands of our father, one of them went to jail, and our dad is dead. Because it was never the time." Garrett punctuated the word *time* with air quotes. "The time is now."

"Why don't we go in the house, sit down and talk about this, calmly." Harlan slapped Ryder on the back. "I know reliving all those memories is painful for you and Wes. I'm asking you to give us one night to talk about it. To ask and answer questions without judgment." He looked at Garrett. "To heal."

"Fine." Garrett trudged up the stairs and stood face-to-face with their mother.

Ryder wrapped a protective arm around her, pulling her closer. His brother may be angry for the lies she told, but he refused to allow anyone to yell at her. He'd never seen his brother show aggression toward anyone before tonight, proving to Ryder that not knowing hurt almost as much as living through the nightmare.

"Mom, I love you, but I need you to make me understand."

"I'll do my best."

Garrett's eyes narrowed at Ryder, letting him know he posed no threat to their mother. He dropped his arm from her shoulder and allowed Garrett to walk her inside.

"Where's Wes?" Ryder asked.

"In the house." Harlan held the door open for them. "He's been here all afternoon."

The six of them spent the next couple hours talking over bottles of water instead of beer. His mother explained her affair, although she never named their uncle. Neither he nor Wes did either. As she said in her letter, who and why didn't matter.

She walked them through the twelve steps of recovery and even gave them information on Al-Anon meetings… the program for friends and family members of alcoholics. She read them the *Serenity Prayer* and the six of them asked God to grant them the serenity to accept the things they couldn't change, the courage to change the things they could and the wisdom to know the difference.

As he drove away from the house, his heart told him there was one last thing he needed to do before he could move forward with his life. Chelsea needed to hear the truth. For them to ever have a real relationship, she needed to know he hadn't killed his father. He wanted their lives together to begin with absolute honesty.

Ryder pulled into her driveway. He hadn't bothered to call ahead. He'd spent fifteen minutes driving around trying to find the right words to explain what he'd done. He'd never told anyone he'd taken the blame for his mother. Tori had been there and had been part of the cover-up. But they hadn't discussed it. He'd refused to. Now he had to talk about it.

He raised his hand to knock on the door when it opened. "I heard you pull in. Is everything okay?"

"It will be. May I come in?"

Chelsea stepped aside and that was when he noticed she wore only an oversize T-shirt. Nothing else. Every curve of her full breasts was visible beneath the thin cotton. Her nipples grew before his eyes, puckering the fabric around them. The clock on the far wall showed a quarter past two. "I didn't realize how late it was. I guess I stayed at Harlan's longer than I thought. Did I wake you?"

"Yes, but I don't mind. Tell me what happened." She walked toward the living room, her hips swaying ever so slightly with each step. "Did you see your mother?" she asked as she tucked her bare legs under her bottom on the couch.

Ryder nodded as he sat beside her, struggling to find the words he needed to say. "My mom and my brothers— all of them—were there. We had some difficult conversations, but it was good. There were a lot of questions and just as many answers, but it's finally over. I think we may have come out a little stronger because of it. Which brings me to why I'm here."

Ryder willed himself to continue as every nerve ending in his body went on high alert.

Chelsea's breathing slowed to the point he wondered if she held her breath. "Please don't keep me in suspense."

He ran his palms back up and down his thighs. *You can do this, Ryder.* He swallowed hard when she shifted her legs and exposed more bare skin. "I want a future with you, Chelsea. And in order for that to happen, there can't be any secrets between us."

Chelsea reached for his hands, stilling them. "I agree. Is there something you need to tell me?"

Half of him believed she already knew the truth and had just been waiting for him to say the words. The other half feared she'd curse him for throwing his life away to protect his mom. Regardless, he couldn't keep it from her any longer. "My mother was the one who accidentally ran over my father."

"Oh, Ryder, I suspected as much after the way you, Tori and Nate reacted to your mother's letter. What happened?"

"Tori drove me home that night." Ryder's pulse beat frantically in his neck as he attempted to tell Chelsea the story without envisioning what happened. "As we drove onto the ranch we saw my parents fighting outside. We didn't know then what they were fighting about, now we do. Mom was trying to leave, and Dad tried to stop her. He grabbed her and she pushed him away. I jumped out of Tori's car and told my dad to leave her alone, but my mom was already getting behind the wheel. She didn't realize my dad had tripped and fallen behind the truck. As he tried to stand, she backed over him."

Chelsea gasped, covering her mouth. "How awful."

Ryder closed his eyes, trying to picture something, anything other than that night. But nothing came. He opened them, landing on the faint smattering of freckles across Chelsea's collarbone. Freckles. Good. Focus on her freckles.

"Tori leaned on the horn. I'm not sure if the sound frightened my mom or if she realized what she'd done, but she threw the truck in Drive and ran over him again, smashing into the side of the house. I banged on the door, but she had locked it. By the time I broke out the window she had passed out over the steering wheel."

"If it was an accident, why did you confess to it?"

"Because my mom's been arrested before. She has a history of driving under the influence. But no one knew that except me because it happened in another county and we hid it from the family. I figured the courts would be more lenient with me than her. There was no way I could have stood by and watched my own mother get locked up."

"I can understand that…it was a brave thing to do. But weren't you concerned about how your own record would be viewed by the court?"

"Nothing else mattered except protecting my mom. Besides, Tori serving me with divorce papers that day, losing my marriage and the kid I had considered my own destroyed me. Prison—as crazy as it may sound—was a hell of a lot more appealing than staying in Saddle Ridge and cleaning up the mess. I took the coward's way out."

"You were far from a coward." Chelsea drew his hands to her lips and began kissing them. "And I knew you didn't do it."

The weight that had been crushing Ryder's chest lifted for the first time since that night. "You and Harlan were both able to see through our story."

She rose to her knees and wound her arms around his neck. "You made the ultimate sacrifice to protect your mother and gave her a second chance at life. And now you have yours. You are the sweetest, most beautiful man I've ever known."

Chelsea pressed her lips against his, fervently urging his mouth open with her tongue. His fingertips grazed bare flesh as they gripped her waist. He tugged her on top of him, her bare bottom straddling his thighs. As much as he wanted to continue kissing her, he needed to see her body. All of it. He broke their kiss and as if sensing his desire, she lifted her shirt over her head, exposing her nakedness to him. This was the raw Chelsea he'd been longing to see since day one. Completely bare before him…for him.

"Make love to me," she purred in his ear. "Make love to me until neither one of us can move."

Ryder eased Chelsea onto her back and stood before her. She watched him undo every button and he watched her darkened nipples bud harder as he unzipped his jeans. He'd never wanted anything more than he did at this very moment. The throbbing ache that burned inside him had grown to a fevered pitch. Tonight, Chelsea would be his.

Chapter 11

The next morning, Chelsea's body still hummed from Ryder's lovemaking. They'd explored every inch of each other and had gone back for more. Their goodbye kiss an hour ago had the promise of more to come, but neither one of them knew when they'd have the opportunity again. Overnight dates weren't easy to schedule with a child in the house.

She checked the clock on the wall. Peyton would be home in a few hours and she needed to talk to Harlan. Together they could convince Ryder and Bernadine to tell the truth and finally clear his name. Without their confessions, Chelsea and Harlan were left in a difficult position. As officers of the court, they were required to turn them in. But she couldn't do that, and she doubted Harlan could either. The truth had to come from Ryder and Bernadine.

The drive to Harlan and Belle's seemed endless. She knew Ryder wouldn't be thrilled she'd turned to his brother for support, but together they could help them build a strong defense and hopefully Bernadine would never spend a day behind bars.

She turned in to Harlan's ranch, relieved to see his police SUV in the driveway, having forgotten to call first. Normally she wasn't this unprepared. Then again, she'd never been this close to a case before.

"Chelsea, this is a surprise." Harlan rose from one of the rocking chairs on the farmhouse's front porch. "I was just having my morning coffee. Would you like a cup?"

"Um." Chelsea gripped the stair rail for support as she climbed the steps. "Yes, please. Just cream."

It would give her a few extra seconds to organize her thoughts.

"It's non-dairy creamer. Is that all right?"

"That's fine."

"Okay." Harlan eyed her warily. "Are you okay?"

Chelsea nodded. "Great, I just need to talk to you."

Harlan gnawed his bottom lip for a moment, then opened the screen door. "I'll be right back with your coffee."

"Thanks." She wanted to say *take your time* but the quicker she got this over with the better for all parties involved. Although it would have been a lot easier if the people involved weren't related to Harlan.

"Here you go." He handed her a steamy mug a few minutes later and motioned for her to sit in one of the rockers. "I'm assuming this is about Ryder."

Chelsea sipped her coffee, instantly wishing she hadn't. She swallowed the hot liquid and cleared her throat. "It's about Ryder and the night your dad died."

Harlan's body immediately stiffened. "What about it?"

"Ryder told me everything last night." She set the mug on the small table between them. "And I'm hoping between the two of us we can convince him and your mom to tell everyone she was the driver that night and finally clear Ryder's name."

"Wait, what?" Harlan stood. "My mom was driving and not Tori?"

Oh God. This isn't happening. "You didn't know? Ryder told me you knew. He said you never believed his story from that night."

"I didn't. I've always known he wasn't the driver. That left only Mom and Tori. For years I thought it was Tori and I'm ashamed to say I had hoped it was, because who wants to believe their mom ran over their dad, right? The other day I—"

Ryder's Jeep rolled to a stop in front of the porch, startling them both. She hadn't even heard him pull up, and apparently neither had Harlan.

"Chelsea, what are you doing here?" His face paled as he unlatched the gate and walked toward them.

"Why did you take the blame for something you didn't do?" Harlan asked from the top step.

Ryder's eyes narrowed at Chelsea. "Why did you tell him?"

"You told me Harlan had never believed your story

and it was all out in the open now." Chelsea's legs shook as she rose from the rocker. "I thought he knew."

"That's not what I meant when I said you both saw through my story. I never planned on telling Harlan." She saw Ryder's jaw clench. "How could you betray me like this? You didn't even wait twelve hours."

"Betray you?" Dread washed over her. "I went to Harlan so we could build your mom's legal defense."

"Who asked you to?" Ryder attempted to climb the steps, but Harlan blocked him.

"Chelsea didn't tell me anything I didn't already know, and you should have told me when it happened," Harlan said. "All these secrets and lies. Look what it's done to this family."

"How dare you say that to me," Ryder growled. "I protected this family. I sacrificed everything so Mom could get the help she needed. She doesn't remember and she doesn't need to remember."

"Yes, she does if we're ever going to clear your name." Chelsea squeezed between them, afraid one of them might punch the other.

"What the hell are you talking about?"

"Harlan and I know now." Chelsea reached out to touch him, only to have him back away as if she'd wielded a branding iron in his face. "You have to tell the police what really happened that night so you can reclaim your life."

"No, I don't." Ryder hopped down from the porch. "I've already reclaimed mine and I thought you were a part of it. I made the biggest mistake of my life trusting you."

The weight of his words almost caused her knees to buckle. "You can't mean that."

"Oh, I do. Even if I had told my brother, you had no right to come here and discuss it with him."

"Would you have preferred I had gone to the police?"

"That's exactly what you did!" Ryder shouted at her. "He is the police!"

"Stop it!" Harlan held up his hands as if he were directing traffic. "Chelsea had an obligation to report it, Ryder. She came to me because she wanted my help. In my heart I already knew the truth, I just needed confirmation."

"The only reason Chelsea wants to clear my name is to protect her reputation, not mine. Time has already been served for that night." He glared at her, his eyes colder than she'd thought possible. "You're only worried about yourself. Your sworn duty. Your image. You couldn't handle being with someone people think killed their father. Accident or not. It wasn't enough for you to know the truth."

"You're wrong."

Ryder shook his head. "I trusted you because I wanted us to have a chance at a future together. For that to happen, you needed to know who I truly am." Ryder looked at Harlan. "And what about you, brother. Are you going to turn us in?"

"No." Harlan sagged against the railing. "It needs to come from you."

"I am not telling anyone Mom killed our father."

"Oh my God!" Bernadine stood in the middle of the path alongside the house. Her face paled as she blindly reached out for something to grab on to. "It wasn't a dream," she whispered. "I really killed Frank."

Ryder ran to his mother and wrapped an arm around her for support.

Chelsea's heart sank. How long had Bernadine been standing there? "Mrs. Slade."

"Don't you dare say a word to my mother." Ryder's eyes blazed with fury. "I never want to see you again."

"I called you all here this morning because you asked me to sleep on it." Bernadine Slade stood in the middle of Harlan's living room, next to her husband who'd flown in last night. "Well, I slept on it, but my decision hasn't changed. I'm turning myself in tomorrow. Please don't try to talk me out of it and I don't want to see any tears from any of you."

"Mom." Ryder crossed the room and stood before her. The woman he'd always seen as strong even during her weakest moments seemed so fragile in front of him now. "I will never agree with your decision, but I respect it."

Staring the unknown in the face for the second time terrified him. He didn't know what his punishment would be this time, but he'd take whatever the courts gave him if it meant they would never have to speak, think or talk about that night ever again.

His mother placed her hand against his cheek and wiped away his tears with her thumb. "I will do everything in my power to make sure nothing happens to you and Tori. You've already lost so much, I can't bear to see you lose any more."

"Then don't do this, Mom," Ryder pleaded. "We just got you back. Don't leave us again. Please."

"Shh, it will be okay." She smiled. "I want us to celebrate Wes and Jade today as we had planned, because I don't know if I'll be able to attend their wedding next weekend. Let's enjoy today and not worry about tomorrow. It will come soon enough."

Tori reached for Ryder's hand and gave it a squeeze. "It's out of our control now."

"I know."

"When this is all over—" his mother patted his cheek "—I want to see you and Chelsea back together."

Tori scoffed beside him. "Good Lord, I hope he doesn't."

"Now you listen to me." Bernadine leaned across Ryder and waggled her finger. "Who do you think you are meddling in his life. He can date whoever he wants, whenever he wants, and he doesn't need you telling him otherwise."

Ryder covered his face and laughed. "Pot meet kettle. Kettle meet pot."

"What's that supposed to mean?" Tori asked.

"It means I don't need either one of you meddling in my... I don't even know what to call it anymore except that it's over. Chelsea and I are over."

"I know you want someone to blame. Life is easier when you can box everything up and put it away when you don't need it. The problem with that is when something is your fault, you can't put it away. You have to live with it and deal with it. I love you, Ryder, with all my heart, but your biggest mistake was covering for me in the first place. That's what this all comes down to. I love you for wanting to protect me, but that wasn't your job. I should have been protecting you. And that's my fault. I wasn't there for you when you needed me most."

"Mom—"

"I'm not finished."

Ryder groaned. He didn't care what his mother had to say, there was no going back to Chelsea. He couldn't be with someone who didn't love him for him. He didn't need someone always trying to fix him or improve him. He needed someone to accept him with all his flaws.

"At least tell me why you're so mad at Chelsea. Because from where I'm sitting she was only trying to do the right thing. You needed to clear your name."

"She only wanted to clear my name for her benefit. So people didn't look at her and wonder how she could be with a man who killed his father."

"What's wrong with that?" his mother asked. "She has a child. What woman in her right mind wants to bring a man who just got out of prison for killing one of his parents into her and her child's life? I would think if you really loved her, you would want only the best for her and her daughter."

"She kind of does have a point there," Tori said. "She accepted you not knowing you were innocent."

"No, she said she always knew I was innocent."

"She suspected but she didn't know for sure. Just like Harlan didn't. I kept pushing her toward you because I knew you were innocent. But if the situation had been reversed, I probably would've knocked her on her butt for even suggesting it."

"Right on."

"Mom, no one says 'right on' anymore." Ryder laughed.

"Who cares? Where I'm going, we make our own rules."

"Mom, you're not going to jail. Me on the other hand… I'm out on parole. They may put me back in until this is settled."

The thought of spending another second behind bars was enough reason for Ryder to never forgive Chelsea. She'd destroyed everything he'd carefully protected, and there was no going back from that.

Chelsea sat in the grass overlooking the Silver Bells ranch. Harlan and Bernadine had invited her to the Slade family gathering, in hopes Ryder would talk to her after ignoring her calls and text messages. If he'd just give her a chance to explain, he'd realize she hadn't betrayed him.

She scanned the ranch again, wondering if he'd spotted her and hightailed it in the other direction. She hated confronting him in public, but after she'd convinced Dante's owner to sell her the horse yesterday after the man had accepted her name-your-price-offer, both Harlan and Bernadine had thought the grand gesture would change his mind. Now she wasn't so sure. Looking around at all his family, it felt a little too public.

Chelsea watched Peyton and Harlan's daughter, Ivy, sign under a shade tree a few feet away. Two years younger than Missy, Ivy had learned many words when Missy had been a part of the family. Harlan had continued to encourage her to expand her vocabulary so they could always communicate.

"I didn't expect to see you here." Tori's voice caught her by surprise.

"I could say the same about you." Chelsea had wanted to talk to Tori about Ryder yesterday afternoon when she picked up Peyton from her school trip, but in front of the school wasn't the place. She'd contemplated calling, then decided to wait until Monday when they could sit down and talk in person. "For the record, I thought Harlan knew the truth when I told him. Regardless of how it happened, Ryder needs to clear his name."

"Since you're so big on honesty, when are you going to be honest with yourself?" Tori knelt in the grass beside her. "You needed Ryder to clear his name so no one thought you were dating a killer."

"That's a little harsh, don't you think?"

"No, no I don't. Not when you consider what you've done to me, to Ryder? We covered up a crime, destroyed evidence and Ryder perjured himself. You forced that issue, now I'm forcing this one."

"I thought it would help them heal as a family."

"Bullshit. That may have been one of the reasons, but it wasn't the main one. This was about your image. Both yours and Peyton's. And I get that. But don't pretend that was only a small part of it."

Chelsea refused to deny that she cared what other people thought about her or her daughter, but she had more substance than that. "I've worked hard to advance my career and provide a good home for my daughter. You forget I have an extra salary to make up for as a single parent. I'm not getting child support. I can't afford to lose my job."

"There it is. You just proved my point. You were afraid your relationship with Ryder would cost you your job."

Chelsea opened her mouth to argue, then shut it. "Oh my God. You're right, I did." She buried her head in her knees. "I hadn't thought it all the way through. I wanted to help. I swear I did, but yeah, I hated the looks people were giving me at work. I hated losing clients because of my relationship with Ryder."

"Chelsea?" Belle walked over to them. "Ryder arrived a few minutes ago and they're about to bring Dante out. Maybe that will help smooth things over between you two."

"Dante?" Tori asked. "He's here?"

Chelsea rose to her feet and looked around. "I convinced the owner to sell me the horse and Harlan picked him up so we could surprise Ryder. But now I'm having second thoughts about doing this in front of everyone."

"May I have your attention, please." Jade Scott, Wes's fiancée, stood on an overturned apple crate in front of everyone. "Next weekend is the big day for me and my hubby-to-be and while that's special, today is special, too. Bernadine and Ryder are finally back home in Saddle Ridge."

"Too late," Chelsea said.

Ryder's family began clapping while Wes blew everyone's eardrums with his two-fingered whistle.

"Even though we're never promised tomorrow," Jade continued, "we're thankful for every day we have together. And Ryder, we hope you'll consider our offer to join Silver Bells because we'd sure love to have you."

"What was that about?" Chelsea asked Belle.

"Ryder's brothers offered him a percentage of the ranch in exchange for him living and working here."

"That's wonderful. I hope he said yes," Chelsea said before realizing that would leave Tori without her ranch hand. "Tori, I'm sorry. I wasn't thinking."

"No, it's okay. We've already discussed it. I think it's a good idea, too."

"They've asked Harlan a few times, but he's always turned them down," Belle added. "They asked again this morning, and he said he'd do it if Ryder does, making Silver Bells a true Slade ranch."

"I'm sensing there's some hesitation though." Chelsea couldn't imagine any reason why Ryder would pass on such a tremendous opportunity to own part of his family's ranch.

"His stubborn pride is getting in the way." Tori dug a buried stone out of the grass with the toe of her boot. "He appreciates their generosity, but since he can't afford to pay for the shares, he says it makes him feel like a charity case."

"Why doesn't he take the percentage now and put money in as he makes it?" Chelsea said. "He can keep contributing until he's matched what they've paid and then he'll have paid them back. It may take some time, but eventually it will even out."

"Now there's an idea." Tori slapped her thigh. "I wish I had thought of that."

"Maybe you'll have a chance to tell him that later."

Belle nudged Chelsea's arm as Ryder stood before everyone.

"Thank you." Ryder's voice went hoarse and Chelsea wished she could give him the support he needed to deal with the days ahead. "I'm glad to be home. I'm still not sure about working here, but I'm strongly considering it. We'll see what tomorrow brings."

"In the meantime, there's someone here who's been waiting a long time to see you." Bernadine pointed toward the stables where Harlan rode toward him on a sorrel-colored quarter horse.

"Oh my God, Dante!" Ryder ran toward his brother. "That's my horse."

Chelsea covered her mouth to keep from crying as Ryder ran his hand down the animal's coppery-red mane. The horse nodded his head and snorted, and Ryder knew he recognized him. "Can you still count for me, boy?" Ryder rubbed the white blaze that ran along the bridge of the animal's nose. "One, two, three, four." On each count, Dante pawed the ground. "That's my boy." Ryder patted his chest. "That's my Dante."

"I never should have sold him." Bernadine held a tissue to her nose and quickly began walking toward Dylan's house.

"Mom, wait." Ryder started to chase after her. "Mom!"

"I got this." Wes grabbed his arm. "Why don't you go thank the woman responsible for bringing Dante home."

"I don't understand. Isn't Mom responsible?"

Harlan slid from the saddle and handed him the reins. "Chelsea made this all happen."

Belle's not-so-subtle shove in Ryder's direction almost sent Chelsea sailing into Dante.

"He's all yours. He's my way of saying I'm sorry." She held her hand out for the horse to sniff. "Now your family's complete."

She detected a flicker of emotion behind his eyes, before they flashed ice cold once again.

"Thank you. It's a very generous gift, but it doesn't change anything between us." He patted the horse on the neck. "It's good to see you, ol' boy, but you don't belong to me." He handed Chelsea the reins. "You bought him, he's yours."

"No, Ryder. I bought him for you. Please take him. He belongs with you. I don't need anything in return. I just wanted to bring him home."

A long silence fell between them before Ryder nodded. "Thank you." Without any further acknowledgment, he turned his back to her, slid the toe of his boot in the stirrup and swung up into the saddle. He gazed down and for a second she thought he'd say more. Instead, he clicked his tongue as he nudged the horse into a trot. Within seconds, they were gone. And so was any hope she'd had of winning his heart.

Chapter 12

The following morning after he'd spent the night with his horse in the Silver Bells stables, Ryder saddled Dante and took him out for another ride. Yesterday had been their reacquaintance, today he wanted to see if Dante was still in shape. He and his family had to leave for the police station in a few hours and Ryder needed to keep busy so the worrying about what was to come wouldn't eat away at his gut.

He eased Dante into a canter, and then a run. They flew across the land as if no time had passed between them. Crisp Montana air filled their lungs as they rode toward the ranch's scenic overlook. They slowed to a walk along the ridge, the rustling song of the western larch's deep golden leaves accompanying them.

The tranquility of the ranch would help prepare him

for the days to come. He'd start with notifying his parole officer of his new job and address. Because regardless of what happened to him, the sooner he moved off Free Rein, the better. Tori and Nate had enough to deal with in the upcoming days without him around. He'd complicated their marriage enough as it was. He would continue to work there until he found and trained a suitable replacement, no matter how long it took. After all she'd done for him, he couldn't leave her in a lurch.

Now that he'd started working with the at-risk youth program, he wanted to not only continue his involvement but learn all he could about the program's structure and hopefully one day replicate it. If a program like that had existed when he'd been a kid, maybe he wouldn't have made so many mistakes. And maybe he would've had an adult to turn to for help.

He walked Dante back to the stables, allowing him to cool down. As he dismounted, he thought he saw Chelsea turn the corner, but no one was there. "Oh great, now I'm seeing things." Not that he wanted to see her. After her betrayal, he could never forgive her.

Dante shifted his body abruptly, almost knocking him to the ground. "Hey, watch it, bub." When the horse bumped him again, he reached for his halter and stared into his eyes. "You can hit me all you want, but I'm not chasing after her. I'm grateful she returned you to me, but it ends there."

A few hours later, he stood beside his brothers on Harlan's front porch in a borrowed suit and tie, waiting for their mother to come outside.

Wes patted him on the back. "This is what she wants.

We've hired the best attorneys and we just have to hold on to each other and stand by her."

After decades of dysfunction, his family had finally come together as a solid unit. While he wished it hadn't taken his mother's legal drama to do it, he'd never felt closer to his brothers.

"I've made a decision." Ryder tugged at his tie to loosen it a bit. "If Harlan is still willing to join Silver Bells, then I am, too. I'd be honored to work alongside each of you."

"I'm in." Harlan grinned. "It looks like the Slade brothers are in business together."

"That's awesome!" Dylan slapped him on the back. "We couldn't be happier."

"You couldn't be happier about what?" their mother asked from the doorway.

"Ryder and Harlan are the newest partners of the Silver Bells Ranch," Garrett said.

"It's about damn time!" His mother stomped her foot, causing them to laugh.

Despite the fear Ryder knew grew within her each passing second, his mother was genuinely happy for them. He just hoped this wasn't the last time they were this happy as a family.

The walk to their cars reminded him of the night he turned himself in. One by one they pulled out of Harlan's driveway like a funeral procession on their way to the sheriff's department. He rode in the back seat of their attorney's SUV with his mother on one side and Tori on the other. Nate had wanted to drive her, but Tori refused to leave Missy with anyone except him.

As the SUV came to a stop in the parking lot, his mother gave his hand three quick squeezes before opening the door and climbing out, without bothering to wait for assistance. She'd made up her mind and nothing was going to get in her way.

Ryder climbed out after her and buttoned his suit jacket. This was the moment he had feared would come, and even though Chelsea had set the entire thing in motion, he couldn't help wishing she was by his side as he walked through the sheriff's department doors. His family had never been stronger, and he loved her for that. He laughed to himself. Of all times to realize he loved Chelsea Logan. He just couldn't be with her. Not until he knew he had a future to offer her.

Chelsea watched the entire Slade saga play out on the news and in the courtroom over the last two weeks. While it was still too soon to know Bernadine's fate, all charges against Ryder and Tori had been dropped yesterday and Ryder's record had been expunged.

Tori had forgiven her, crediting Ryder's mother for helping her realize her motives hadn't been selfish or malicious. If only Ryder had seen it that way. She had reached out to him a few times but hadn't heard back. Tori had offered to intervene but the last thing either one of them needed was more interference from an outside party.

That didn't mean she'd given up. The longer they'd been apart, the more she realized she truly loved him. And she was tired of waiting for him to come to his senses. She clicked off the TV with the remote and grabbed her jacket and keys. It was Saturday afternoon and Peyton had gone to a friend's house for the day. After cleaning everything in sight and reorganizing her kitchen cabinets…twice, she needed to get out of the house. Even if it was just for a ride around the block. She had to do something, anything to get Ryder out of her head.

She had fully intended to drive to Flathead Lake, but instead found herself turning in to the Silver Bells Ranch. She didn't know if Ryder would be there, but she had to at least try. Tori had told her he'd already found someone to replace him at Free Rein and he'd officially moved off her ranch. Slowing to a crawl in front of the stables, she scanned for any sign of Ryder. There were a handful of cars and four-wheelers parked nearby, but she had no idea what he drove these days since the Jeep had belonged to Nate.

She braked near the stable entrance and glanced around for someone to ask where she might find him. She didn't need to look far. The building's shadowy interior couldn't disguise the purposeful stride of the man walking toward her.

Within seconds he reached the car. Then he opened the driver-side door and offered her his hand. She shut off the engine and accepted, relishing the feel of his skin against hers. Two weeks had been too long to go without a single touch from him.

"How did you know where to find me?"

"I—I didn't." She stared up at him, melting in the warmth that emanated from his smile. She'd expected instant rejection or at the very least residual anger.

Not…affection. "Tori told me you moved here so I thought I'd take a chance and stop by."

"I was planning to call you soon." He released her hand, burying his in his pockets. "I apologize for not returning your calls, but I couldn't until I knew what my future held."

"I saw on the news yesterday that they dropped the charges. I'm happy for you." Chelsea wanted to hug him, but his posture made her think twice. "I never meant to hurt you."

"You didn't." He closed his eyes and shook his head. When he opened them again, the pain of the past had faded, leaving only sincerity behind. "I not only hurt myself, I hurt them, too. I'm just sorry it took me so long to realize it. Now we can finally heal. And that never would have been possible without you. You pushed and pushed—"

"I pushed too hard, I'm so sorry."

Ryder cupped her chin. "Sweetheart, don't be. If you hadn't, my family wouldn't be here together. I realize now that you wanting to clear my name wasn't just for you, or me or Peyton. It was for all of us."

Chelsea reached for his hands and pressed them against her heart. It pounded so hard she was certain he could feel it beneath his palms. "I made a lot of mistakes, Ryder. I put too much emphasis on what other people thought. I lost us and what mattered most in the process. Can you ever forgive me?"

"I already have." He kissed her softly on the mouth. "You have such an amazing capacity to help people, and I couldn't see what I had until I lost it. Do you think you might be willing to give this fool of a man a second chance to love you? Because I would really love to build a life with you and Peyton."

Chelsea had never imagined loving someone as much as she loved Ryder. The man tested her at every turn, and that made her fight for him even more. "I can't think of anything that would make me happier. I love you, Ryder Slade."

Epilogue

It was the third Saturday in May and Chelsea still couldn't believe that in less than half an hour she'd walk down the aisle toward her groom.

"You look pretty, Mommy." Peyton signed as she spoke.

"You're stunning, my love." Chelsea's mother fastened the headpiece to Chelsea's hair and kissed her softly on the cheek. "I've never seen a more beautiful bride."

"Thank you, but I'm sure all mothers say that to their daughters." She signed, "One day I'll say it to mine."

"I can't wait to get married." Peyton sang as she spun around in her pale pink flower girl dress. "I want to marry a man just like Ryder."

And Chelsea hoped she did. Just not for another twenty or thirty years.

The door to the Silver Bells Ranch bridal suite opened, and Jade popped her head in. "Are you ready to do this, soon-to-be Mrs. Ryder Slade?" She giggled.

"Yes, I am, Mrs. Weston Slade." Chelsea always hated being an only child and loved that she suddenly had four of the sweetest sisters-in-law a bride could ask for.

Tori handed her a bouquet of classic pink roses, white lisianthus and silver brunia, wrapped in a white satin ribbon. "Ryder won't be able to take his eyes off you. I can't believe that's your mother's gown. It looks so fresh and modern."

"You've always been fresh and modern, haven't you, Mom?"

"Fresh, modern and four months pregnant when I walked down the aisle," her mother added.

Chelsea may only be three months along, but she and Peyton had a surprise about the pregnancy to tell Ryder and their guests during the ceremony. She didn't know who was more excited about her pregnancy…she, Peyton or Ryder. It would be an adjustment for Peyton to have a hearing sibling, but she had faith her daughter would find the right balance. She'd already started interning with Dr. Lydia Presley for a few hours on the weekends. There was nothing her daughter couldn't do.

Jade led the way to the Silver Bells Lodge as a white horse-drawn carriage pulled up out front. It paid to have a Los Angeles wedding planner living on-site. Her father lifted Peyton into the carriage before helping Chelsea. "My beautiful daughter, I'm so proud of you."

The slow carriage ride through the ranch gave her

a chance to give thanks for all the blessings that had come into her life. When she'd moved to Saddle Ridge almost two years ago, she'd wondered if she'd even have the time to make friends, let alone meet the man of her dreams.

As they crested the final hill, the wedding gazebo came into view. The gazebo Dylan Slade had built for his bride and the place every Slade brother had married.

Her father helped her, Tori and Peyton out of the carriage, as Dylan escorted her mother to the front row. Chelsea hadn't wanted a large wedding party. She only needed her daughter and Tori to stand up with her. Ryder had asked Harlan to be his best man...and Wes his ring-bearing groomsman. It was just one more unconventional addition to their already crazy lives. And she wouldn't want it any other way.

A lone harpist began to play Wagner's "Bridal Chorus" as her father offered his arm and they stepped onto the white satin runner together. She checked over her shoulder and mouthed *I love you* to Peyton. This was it. This was their fairy-tale ending in front of their family and friends.

Chelsea stopped as they reached the front row and pulled two roses from her bouquet, handing one to her mother and the other to Ryder's mother. The court had found Bernadine Slade not guilty on the grounds she had been under extreme emotional distress in the events leading up to the accident and that Frank Slade had been intoxicated. His mistress of all people had taken the stand in Bernadine's defense and confirmed his alcoholism.

Slipping back beside her father, she continued to the gazebo where Ryder, handsome as the devil in his dark dress denims, crisp white shirt, black vest and cowboy hat, just about made her heart beat out of her chest.

"Who gives this woman to be married to this man?" Reverend Grady asked as an interpreter signed for Peyton and Missy.

"Her mother and I do." Chelsea's father joined her hands with Ryder's and kissed her on the cheek.

"Here we are!" Chelsea squeaked. "I can't believe this is it."

"I love you so much." Ryder squeezed her hands.

"I love you, too."

"Hey, you two," Reverend Grady interrupted. "You keep this up and you'll put me out of a job." Their wedding guests laughed as he continued. "Ladies and gentlemen, it is my pleasure to officiate over my sixth Slade wedding. And I say sixth because I married Harlan and Belle twice. Over the past two years, I have come to love this family as if they were my own. Heck, I'm usually at one of their houses for Sunday dinners." That got another laugh from the crowd. "The point I'm trying to make is, the larger I've seen this family grow, the more love I've seen not only from them, but for them. Let me be the first to thank you for coming as we gather together to join this man and woman in holy matrimony. Ryder and Chelsea have chosen to write their own vows."

"Chelsea," Ryder began. "I've never been a man of many words, but the day I first saw you and you took my breath away, I didn't want to stop talking to you. You came into my life like a bull in a china shop."

"Oh gee, thanks." Chelsea didn't know if she should kiss or smack him.

"Give me a minute, it gets better. Keep in mind I'm a cowboy, we think in terms of bulls. What I'm trying to say is you crashed through the door of my heart so fast and so hard, some days I didn't know which end was up. You challenge me as much as you excite me, and I hope that never changes. I look forward to spending every day of the rest of my life with you as my wife and Peyton as my daughter." Ryder gestured for Peyton to join them. Releasing Chelsea's hand, he turned to her daughter and signed, "I promise to always be there for you, for as long as I'm alive. I love you and I'm honored to be your father."

"I love you, too." Peyton threw her arms around Ryder as he bent to kiss her cheek. Taking her hand in his, he faced their guests and motioned for the interpreter to stand in front of him so Peyton could see what he was about to say.

"This is my daughter. With her mother's permission and Peyton's blessing, I am adopting her and offering to give her the Slade family name. She is my child, body, heart and soul."

He gave Peyton another hug as Chelsea swiped at her eyes with the tissue Tori handed her. She had known Ryder would make the announcement, she just hadn't known when. She adored that he'd included Peyton in his vows.

"I don't know how to top that." Chelsea gave her

daughter a hug and kiss before taking Ryder's hands in hers. "I don't have a bull analogy, but I thought you were quite the stud when I first saw you. I may have even drooled a little. Looks aside, I quickly learned that you put everyone else above yourself, regardless of the cost. I've met many honorable men in my profession, but I've never met one as honorable as you. You put love and family above all else and I couldn't ask for a better man to call my husband and the father of my children." Chelsea held out her hand for Peyton to join them once again. Placing her daughter's hands and Ryder's on her belly, she signed, "It's no secret I'm pregnant. But Peyton has something special she wants to tell you about our baby." She nodded to Peyton.

"Mommy's having twins. A boy and a girl." Her daughter sang loudly.

Ryder dropped to his knees and stared up at her, tears streaming down his cheeks. "Twins?" He signed, "I'm the luckiest man alive." He hugged Peyton with one arm and tried to hug Chelsea's belly with the other.

She didn't know whether to laugh or cry as Wes and Harlan pulled Ryder to his feet.

"I think we need to get wedding rings on these two before we run out of tissues," Reverend Grady intervened. "May I have the rings please?"

Wes handed Chelsea's ring to Ryder and he slid it on her finger. "Chelsea Abigail Logan, with this ring I profess my never-ending love and commitment to you."

Wes handed Ryder's ring to Peyton who helped Chelsea slide it on Ryder's finger. "Ryder Thomas Slade, with this ring I profess my never-ending love and commitment to you."

"Ladies and gentlemen, by the power vested in me by the state of Montana and the Lord above, I present to you, Ryder and Chelsea Slade. You may kiss your bride."

Their guests erupted into applause and shouts, but the only words she heard, the only words that mattered were Ryder's. "I love you, with all my heart." His lips crashed against hers and in that moment, she had truly become his.

For their first dance, a pianist accompanied by a cellist played Christina Perri's "A Thousand Years," and Chelsea, Peyton and Ryder danced together as they had eight months ago. Chelsea loved the way Ryder included her daughter in almost everything they did. They still had their private moments that called for a babysitter, but most of the time they enjoyed just being a family. If anyone had told her last year that she'd be a member of the biggest family in town with two more on the way, she would've bet a million dollars against it. All the money in the world couldn't buy the happiness she'd found in Ryder Slade.

She'd never felt incomplete, but having Ryder in their lives completed her and Peyton. Her daughter finally had a father. A man she looked up to and respected. A man who understood not only her needs but her words. That alone was something most hearing people took for granted. The challenges of blended families with deaf children were greater when so few hearing people spoke sign language. And while Ryder may not be

Prince Charming, he came pretty darn close. She had no doubt in her mind they would live happily ever after in their new house on the Silver Bells Ranch with Marmalade, Jam Jam, Dante…and Cactus, too.

* * * * *

When Shania Stewart tells Deputy Daniel Tallchief that
he needs to lighten up with his wild younger sister,
the handsome lawman doesn't know whether to
ignore her or kiss her. But Shania knows.
It's going to take a carefully crafted lesson plan
to tutor this cowboy in love.

Read on for a sneak preview of
The Lawman's Romance Lesson,
the next great book in USA TODAY *bestselling author*
Marie Ferrarella's Forever, Texas miniseries.

Shania flushed as she raised her eyes toward Daniel. "I don't usually babble like this."

Daniel found the pink hue that had suddenly risen to her cheeks rather sweet. The next second, he realized that he was staring. Daniel forced himself to look away. "I hadn't noticed."

"Yes, you had," Shania contradicted. "But I think that it's very nice of you to pretend that you hadn't." When she heard Daniel laugh softly to himself, she asked him, "What's so funny?" before she could think to stop herself.

"I'm not accustomed to hearing the word *nice* used to describe me," he admitted.

Didn't the man have any close friends? Someone to bolster him up when he was down on himself? "You're kidding."

The lopsided smile answered her before he did. "Something else I'm not known for."

She pretended that he was a student and she did a quick assessment of the man before her. "You know you're being very hard on yourself."

"Not hard," he contradicted. "Just honest."

She had no intention of letting this slide. If he had been one of her students, she would have done what she could to raise his spirits—or maybe it was his self-esteem that needed help.

"Well, I think you're nice—and you do have a sense of humor."

"If you say so," Daniel replied, not about to dispute the matter. He had a feeling that arguing with Shania would be pointless. "But just so you know, I'm not about to chuck my career and become a stand-up comedian."

She grinned at his words. "See, I told you that you had a sense of humor," she declared happily.

Don't miss
The Lawman's Romance Lesson *by Marie Ferrarella, available April 2019 wherever*
Harlequin® *Special Edition books and ebooks are sold.*

www.Harlequin.com

Looking for more satisfying love stories
with community and family at their core?

Check out **Harlequin® Special Edition**
and **Love Inspired®** books!

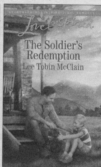

New books available every month!

CONNECT WITH US AT:

Facebook.com/groups/HarlequinConnection

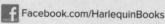 Facebook.com/HarlequinBooks

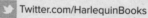 Twitter.com/HarlequinBooks

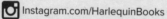 Instagram.com/HarlequinBooks

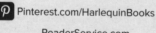 Pinterest.com/HarlequinBooks

ReaderService.com

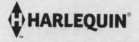

**ROMANCE WHEN
YOU NEED IT**